Covenant Mission

T.L. Smith
with Lauren M. Smith

Bible quotes taken from *The New American Bible* translated from the original languages with critical use of all the ancient sources. World Catholic Press, a division of Catholic Book Publishing Corp. Canada. Copyright 1987.

Publication Date: November 22, 2020, Solemnity of Our Lord Jesus Christ, King of the Universe

ISBN 13: 978-0-9862613-3-6

E-BOOK ISBN 13: 978-0-9862613-4-3

Black & white sketches and painting of the Holy Trinity
by Lulu Liddi

Painting of the Guardian of the Trumpets with the
Ark of the Covenant
by Katie Schmid

Final Edit
by Michele C. Wills

Other books by T.L. Smith

The Great Plan and the Perpetual Rose

The Final Battle for the Kingdom

To our Father,

who art in Heaven…

We exist in His thought in Eternity and entered time through cooperation.

I give you praise, Father, Lord of Heaven and Earth, for although you have hidden these things from the wise and learned, you have revealed them to the childlike. Yes, Father, such has been your gracious will.

— Luke 10:21

Table of Contents

Prologue · xi

Chapter 1 The Father's Gaze ·1
Chapter 2 First Trumpet ·3
Chapter 3 Covenant ·6
Chapter 4 E-Scroll· ·9
Chapter 5 Into Time · 12
Chapter 6 Mother of My Lord · · · · · · · · · · · · · · · · · · 16
Chapter 7 Connection · 21
Chapter 8 Stone Tablets· 26
Chapter 9 The Father's Children · · · · · · · · · · · · · · · · ·30
Chapter 10 Second Trumpet ·34
Chapter 11 The Fiery Pit · 36
Chapter 12 Ripple· ·40
Chapter 13 Manna ·45
Chapter 14 The Father's Weapon· · · · · · · · · · · · · · · · · ·50
Chapter 15 Third Trumpet ·53
Chapter 16 The Rod · 55
Chapter 17 The Living Promise · · · · · · · · · · · · · · · · · · 59
Chapter 18 Bearers of a Great Treasure · · · · · · · · · · · · · 62
Chapter 19 Man of Peace · 69
Chapter 20 Descending· ·72
Chapter 21 The Father's Love · · · · · · · · · · · · · · · · · · · 75

Chapter 22   Fourth Trumpet ·78
Chapter 23   Which Eternity? ·82

              From NASA to the Priesthood · 87
              The Great Warning · 89
              Prayer of Consecration to Jesus through Mary · · · · · · · · · 93
              Prayer for Spiritual Communion · 95
              Best Prayer For The End Times Psalm 91 · · · · · · · · · · · · · ·97
              Seven Trumpets of the Bible · 99
              Glossary · 103
              Bibliography · 109

Prologue

That's one small step for man, one giant leap for mankind.

— NEIL ARMSTRONG

WHO IS MAN? Where does his identity come from? What is his reason for being? The answers to these 3 Ws are found in Genesis – the first book of the Bible. We are man. Our identity lies in our relationship with God as His children. He created us to know, love, and serve Him so that we can be with Him in Heaven when we die. He gives us all we need to reach that goal. Somewhere along the line, we forgot what we were created for. We used the resources given to us by God for our selfish desires rather than to obtain a place in Heaven. Saint Paul tells us that we all form one body, the Mystical Body of Christ. Each members' actions and thoughts in the Mystical Body of Christ either obtains grace or loses grace for the body as a whole. Today, the loss of grace and attacks on the Mystical Body are so portentous that we are spiraling toward the demise of our true identity as children of God.

Can we turn the tide on this cycle of destruction and find our way back to God? The question may not be if we can, but if we will? The choice is ours. The only way to restore our lost identity is to acknowledge that God exists and repent for our offenses against Him. The search for meaning must come from moving upward. This movement can only come through true love. As the saying goes, "love exists in Eternity" but hate also exists in Eternity. The path to heaven is up and there is love in Eternity and the path to hell is down and there is hate in Eternity.

The story you are about to read may be science fiction, but its message is real. God is love and God is the end goal. At the end of our earthly life, we will be judged on how much we used and abused that love. This alone will determine if you and I have made a giant leap - toward an Eternity in Heaven or an Eternity in Hell.

Then I saw the Mother of God, who said to me, [...] "I gave the Savior to the world; as for you, you have to speak to the world about His great mercy and prepare the world for the Second Coming of Him who will come, not as a merciful Savior, but as a just Judge. O, how terrible is that day! Determined is the day of justice, the day of divine wrath. The Angels tremble before it. Speak to souls about this great mercy while it is still the time for [granting] mercy. If you keep silent now, you will be answering for a great number of souls on that terrible day. Fear nothing. Be faithful to the end. I sympathize with you."[1]

---

1 *Diary of Saint Maria Faustina Kowalska*, p. 264, #635.

CHAPTER 1

The Father's Gaze

All those who call me by the name of Father, even
if only once, will not perish, but will be sure of
their eternal life among the chosen ones.[2]

THE PROPHETS OF OLD, THE elect, the chosen ones, and the Angels con-
vened in the Grand Palace. Twelve gates, each made from a single pearl,
enclosed the palace. Which, fashioned from pure gold, glistened like a
transparent crystal. There was great excitement as they waited for the Lady.

"Here comes Our Lady," said one.

The Lady wore a pure white gown of Heavenly beauty, more irides-
cent than the moon. As she passed the audience, each person bowed
before her. She glided gracefully over the emerald floor and stepped
up to the throne where her Father awaited her. She observed her Father
gazing at the eye of a needle as she approached Him. It was through this
opening that He could look upon Earth after the death of His Son.

He gave a sorrowful sigh and said, "Oh, my people, what have I done
to you? How have I offended you?"

"Forgive them Father, for they are ignorant of your love," the Lady
gently responded.

With another heartfelt sigh, He spoke wistfully, "What can I do?
The people on Earth are not listening, and nature itself is calling out

---

2 *The Father Speaks to His Children,* p. 27 and 30.

to destroy them. My heart is full of sorrow when I think of what will become of them. I am sending you again among them, and I want you to give them my message. It is peace that they must seek, and this peace must begin in each of their hearts. They can still turn things around, but they *must* heed the message of Heaven."

"Yes, Father, I shall travel through time to convey your message to them."

"Above all, tell them that I think of them, that I love them, and that I want to give them eternal happiness. Despite their unbelief, I always remain close to them."[3]

"If they only knew…if only their hearts were not so hardened, then they would know that you are their God and Father," His daughter responded.

"I will have to give them a warning to let them know that they are in danger. It is not I that condemn them, but man condemns himself through his own faults. I have signaled the Guardian of the Trumpets to sound the first blast."

---

3 Ibid, p. 49.

CHAPTER 2

First Trumpet

The seven Angels who were holding the seven

trumpets prepared to blow them.

— REVELATION 8:6

AT THE PINNACLE OF THE East Wing of Eternity, stood a tall, awe-inspiring Angel. He cupped his hands to his mouth and imparted a blast that resounded from Heaven to the universe. It was the first trumpet warning signifying the arrival of the Apocalypse. Without delay, the Nine Choirs of Angels met to discuss the impending events. The Nine Choirs of Angels were comprised of three groups: The Angels of Pure Contemplation, the Angels of the Cosmos, and the Angels of the World. God assigns each group of Angels specific roles and tasks. The Angels with the highest level of knowledge and awareness of God are the Angels of Pure Contemplation.

One of the Angels of Pure Contemplation, a Seraphim, entered Earth to observe the proceeding of a decisive court case. The case of Mr. William Barron vs. the 9th Circuit court. Mr. Barron is suing the state for the wrongful death of his unborn child. The state allowed his girlfriend to abort the child without his consent. He is fighting for the rights of fathers regarding their unborn children's right to life. The Seraphim came to the court just as the plaintiff's attorney claimed, "victim of assault," while presenting an ultrasound of the six-month-old baby.

Outside the courthouse, pro-abortionist demonstrators shouted, "My body! My choice! My body! My choice!" Inside the courthouse an uproar ensued between those who held opposing views on the controversial topic of abortion. The judge pounds the gavel on the mahogany stained desk, "Order in the court! Order in the court!"

The defense attorney shouted, "Her right to privacy, based on the right to non-interference and the principle of autonomy, takes precedence over the fetus' existence. The ultrasound is not relevant to the case since the woman has a right to choose what she thinks is best for her health, and like the people outside are saying: It is her body." Everyone looked at the ultrasound of the six-month-old fetus. Many were scratching their heads as disputes erupted among the jury members. Some said, "What is that?" The judge pounded his gavel, but it only increased the commotion.

It was the plaintiff's attorney's turn to speak. He stood up and said, "Yes, like the crowd is shouting out there: Her body! Her choice! And she made her choice; and as a result we now have two bodies here. Her body and the baby's body. The baby has a right to life, just as you and I who have been born have that right. That is what this father is fighting for: his daughter who was in her mother's womb." Again, rumbling filled the court.

The Seraphim stood behind a cartoon columnist. The cartoonist was drawing the judge hitting the gavel and showing confusion in the court. He titled the scene, "Abortion case causes more controversy." The Seraphim looked over at the cartoonist's Guardian Angel. His Guardian Angel said, "His thoughts are clouded by the evil one and his minions, so he is unable to see what is happening in the court." The Seraphim and the Guardian Angel had an idea. They inspired the cartoonist with an image for him to think about.

The cartoonist looked at what he had drawn and shook his head. He ripped the page off the pad and crumpled it. Suddenly, a thought came to him and he started to draw again. After he finished, he looked at the drawing and thought, *why didn't I see this before? It's so obvious.* The Angels looked over the man's shoulders to see the final drawing. He drew a very proud caveman lovingly touching his very pregnant wife's stomach. Above the caveman's head was a thought bubble showing how he will teach his young son how to hunt and spear a fish. On the right side of the caveman's image was the scene inside the courtroom. Everyone was looking at the ultrasound that showed a figure of a baby, curled up in its mother's womb, sucking its thumb. Above the people's head was a thought bubble that said, "What is that?" Underneath the cartoon image of the caveman and the court, the cartoonist wrote: *Modern Intelligence? Have we progressed?*

The Seraphim observed other similar court cases occurring on Earth. He witnessed judges who were not upholding either the Eternal or the Natural Laws. The people of Earth are now calling good 'evil' and evil 'good'. They no longer allow the Eternal Laws in their buildings. What is written by God is being rejected by the children of Earth.

The first Angel announced in a loud voice, "Fear God and give Him glory, for His time has come to sit in judgment. Worship Him who made Heaven and Earth and sea and springs of water."

— REVELATION 14:7

CHAPTER 3

Covenant

"...THREE, TWO, ONE...WE HAVE LIFT OFF!" said a voice from the Command Center in Houston.

The three astronauts braced themselves for a rough ride as the space shuttle, Covenant, lifted off the launch pad. Within seconds, Covenant shot straight through the clouds. Breathing became harder as their bodies were pressed against their seats by the force of gravity. This lasted for a few minutes, but it felt much longer. Moments later, the rockets attached to the shuttle burned out and fell away to Earth, making the ride smoother.

Hours later, Covenant successfully reached its intended destination in space; Captain Jack Benson shut off the engine. Astronaut Caleb Goldberg, the second in command, released the empty fuel tank, sending it down to Earth. The force of gravity was gone, and the astronauts were able to move freely.

"Wow! What a ride!" Bill Smith, the chief engineer, said as he unbuckled his seat belt and floated toward a window in the flight deck. His brown eyes widened as he took in the magnificent view. Earth looked like a small marble with swirls of blue and white.

The three astronauts peered out the window and took in the majestic canvas of space before them.

"The universe looks so amazing from up here!" exclaimed Caleb as he put on his eyeglasses to get a clearer look.

"It certainly does," Bill agreed, a broad smile spreading across his weathered face.

"You want to see something? Look out there. Earth is the only planet that can sustain life. If Earth were positioned any closer to the sun, we would all burn to death; any further away and we would freeze. Even the percentage of gases in the oxygen level must be just right for Earth to sustain life. How could a blast or an explosion have done all of that? For me, it's God who put all of this into place when He created this world —this universe we live in."

Bill raised his eyebrows as he eyed Caleb dubiously, "Those are good points. You sure have deep thoughts in that head of yours."

Caleb said, "I wonder what's happening on Earth right now."

"I know," said Bill. "Makes me glad to be up here, away from all the problems: changing government and threat of a nuclear war."

While Caleb and Bill were talking, Jack updated Command Center on their safe arrival to Earth's orbit. He turned to Caleb and Bill and said, "Well, let's not forget we have a mission here, men. Let's get that spy satellite fixed before we have another world war."

"Yes, Sir!" they exclaimed.

The Covenant was launched into space so that the United States could fix their reconnaissance satellite. It had malfunctioned a few weeks ago at a very critical time—when World War III could have broken out at any moment. Without the satellite fixed, the United States will be at a disadvantage and not able to monitor events happening in other countries.

The three astronauts were chosen for this mission for the skill sets they each possessed. Bill, a tough-looking cowboy, had unkempt brown hair, a squared jawline, and piercing brown eyes. Looking at him, one would never have guessed he was an engineer who had numerous experiences with satellites and could fix nearly anything. Caleb, a mild-mannered, middle-aged man, whose well-groomed appearance contributed to his being mistaken for a college professor had salt-pepper hair neatly combed to one side and large, wire-rimmed glasses which framed his dark, inquisitive eyes. He is also an engineer as well as an astrophysicist. Jack is six-feet-tall with well-groomed auburn hair which seems to have natural blond highlights. Blessed not only with physical beauty, but brains as well, he earned a Ph.D. in astrophysics and chemistry at the same time. He ranked at the top of his class in the United States Naval Academy and was their best fighter pilot. He had successfully led a team into space once before. His experience qualified him to lead the mission.

"Put on your helmets men, and prepare to check out the satellite," said Jack. "We'll need to video feed this back to Command Center so that they can confirm the damage on their end before we fix it. Let's get to work."

Caleb and Bill were suiting up when Command Center called in. "Jack! A large meteorite is coming your way at lightning speed!!"

Captain Jack rushed to the cockpit not knowing where the meteor was coming from. He reached for the controls to turbo thrust them out of its way. Just as the meteor was about to hit them, a glorious light propelled the colossal meteor away from the space ship. The three astronauts were struck with awe at the light, and for a few moments, they were speechless.

"Do you all see what I am seeing?" Jack said.

"Did that light just push the meteor out of the way?" Caleb asked.

"How did that light propel the huge meteor?" Bill asked, his mouth wide open in disbelief.

"Come in, Jack. Is everyone okay?" came a voice from Command Center.

"This is Jack. The meteor didn't hit us," Jack relayed.

"Come in, Covenant?" Command Center asked.

"This is Jack. Can you hear us, Command Center?" Jack called back. Still no answer.

"Connection might have been damaged somehow by the heat of the meteorite," Caleb said.

They were stranded in space with no communication to Earth.

CHAPTER 4

E-Scroll

THE GREAT LIGHT WHICH PROPELLED the meteorite suddenly changed course and flew toward the window of the shuttle. The light emanated majestic power, physically paralyzing them. As the light faded, the astronauts were able to move again. Before them stood a tall figure with short, red hair, dressed in heavenly robes.

"Fear not! I am an Angel sent by God to guide you on your mission."

Still stunned, the astronauts did not realize they were now kneeling before the Angel. Jack spoke first, "I thought that the light was God Himself. So, you knew we were coming here to fix the satellite?"

"Fixing your satellite will not prevent your world from entering into another war. Fixing your people will. You were sent here to receive a great message for the people of Earth, who are defying God.

"Yes, Earth is preparing for a Great War," Jack said. "What is this message?"

"God is giving you a new mission. First, you need to understand the Ark of the Covenant before you can relay the message to the people of Earth," said the Angel.

"What kind of mission?"

"You will know your mission as you solve the mystery of the Ark of the Covenant. The mystery of the Ark of the Covenant is the answer to save your world from self-destruction. In order to do so, you must understand how the Bible works."

"You want us to find the Ark using our satellite?" asked Bill.

The Angel responded, "No, you will use faith and reason to find the Ark.

Jack looked at Caleb and Bill and asked, "Do either of you know anything about the Ark of the Covenant?"

"I'm Jewish, and the Jewish Bible has three parts: the Torah, The Nevi'im (prophets), and the Ketuvim (writings). I know some things about the Ark in the Torah," replied Caleb.

"Do not worry, the teachings of the Jews are contained in the Old Testament, and the teachings of Jesus are contained in the New Testament. The Christian Bible contains both the Old and the New Testaments," responded the Angel. "Jesus did not do away with the teachings of the old prophets."

"I'm an atheist," said Bill. "But now, I'm not sure what I believe."

"I confess that I'm Catholic, but I stopped practicing my faith in college. You said that God chose *us* to fulfill this mission? Shouldn't He give the message to someone who knows the Bible?" Jack asked the Angel.

"God always chooses the least qualified. You will need to work together to find the greatest symbol that God left for mankind."

Least qualified? Bill thought to himself. *That's funny. We're in space because we're the most qualified yet unqualified to solve this mystery.* He asked the Angel, "Why do we have to solve a mystery if God has all the answers? Why can't you just give us the message, and we'll relay it to Earth?"

"Man always wants a shortcut. Be patient. God always has a plan," the Angel replied.

"Will you provide us with a Bible to use to solve this mystery?" Jack asked.

"Yes; I will also take you into the Old and New Testaments, and you will witness the events related to the Ark of the Covenant."

"Wait a second. I'm Jewish; we don't believe in the New Testament. Are you saying that Jesus Christ is God?" asked Caleb.

"Yes, Jesus is the Son of God who came down from Heaven to die for mankind."

Caleb was speechless, trying to make sense of what he was hearing.

"Soon you will understand. Use the clues in the Bible to solve the mystery of the Ark of the Covenant." The Angel touched the necklace around his neck and showed them the small crystal scroll that hung from the end. "This is an E-Scroll. It can display scenes from the Bible like a movie."

"Can you give us time to discuss this?" Jack asked.

The Angel had a serious look on his face and responded, "Time is of the essence. The sooner you begin your new mission, the sooner you will return to Earth."

It is the LORD who goes before you; he will be with you and will never fail you or forsake you. So do not fear or be dismayed.

— Deuteronomy 5:17

CHAPTER 5

Into Time

JACK MOTIONED TO HIS CREW to get up and they walked several feet away from the Angel to discuss. "I don't think we have a choice but to play along and solve this Ark of the Covenant thing so we can get back home."

"It's looking like that," whispered Bill as he looked back at the Angel.

"If this is from God, we need to do what the Angel tells us," Caleb stated.

Jack turned to the Angel and said, "Well, the first Ark was Noah's, right?"

"Ah, that is very good. That was also a vessel—just like the Ark of the Covenant was—but it carried different things. It will be a part of understanding the Ark of the Covenant later," the Angel said. "For now, I would like you to first take a look at the Ark of the Covenant as it was during Moses' time."

Caleb recalled a story that said Moses built an Ark covered with gold. Before the Angel took them on their journey to the Ark, he wanted to clarify the correlation between the Old and the New Testaments, "The Old Testament gives us a blueprint of God's plan. The New Testament is where God brings His plans to life by fulfilling what He foretold in the Old Testament."

Time reached a standstill as the present moment faded out of view and the bright light from the E-scroll sucked the astronauts into a tunnel-like vacuum transporting them back in time. Seconds later, they were in a tan, leathery tent, where an old man was inspecting three items on a table. A glistening bronze lampstand stood close by, glowing brightly.

They heard the Angel's voice. "Time is of the essence. You have entered into the time of Moses."

"Is this for real?" Caleb questioned.

"That's my line," Bill quipped.

"Yes, you are now in the Old Testament of the Bible," the Angel continued. "When you are present in history, you are only there as an observer. The past has already occurred and cannot be changed."

"So, Moses can't see or hear us?" asked Jack.

"That's right. You are only an observer. I cannot help you find the clues or solve the mystery. You have to work together to understand what you are seeing."

"I still don't understand. You never told us what clues to look for." Bill said.

"You are here to understand the Ark. Just observe," the Angel said. They watched Moses carry two stone tablets toward a veiled door. He pushed the veil aside and entered an inner room. The astronauts followed him as he placed the two stone tablets inside a golden box. Then, Moses went back to the outer room. Next, he grabbed a gold bowl with a lid on it. He opened the lid; inside were round, creamy flakes resembling the tops of mini mushrooms.

He went back into the end of the tent, bowed before the box, and placed the paten with the flakes inside. Again, he left the inner room to retrieve a rod from the table. The rod had flower buds and white blossoms at the top. It fit perfectly in the box.

Amazed at what he was witnessing, Caleb shared the great privilege of what they were seeing, "This inner chamber is the Holy of Holies and the golden box is the Ark of the Covenant. Look at the intricate designs carved into the chest and how the two Angels kneel opposite each other atop the chest, with their elegant wings outstretched, forming a seat upon which the cloud of glory rests. Did you know that the Ark can only be touched by priests? Any other person will die."

"So, this is the Ark of the Covenant. It is a magnificent chest," Bill remarked as he tried to touch the Ark, "Good thing we can't die here."

The Angel warned, "Hang on!" With lightning speed, they found themselves in another time. They were taken to another chamber, but this one was grandiose and fit for a king. Massive stone pillars, spanning thirty feet high, stood in each corner. Velvet curtains hung from the pillars, enclosing the royal chamber. A golden harp leaned against its stand and vivid paintings depicting war and bloodshed hung on the walls. In the center was a canopy bed, built from mahogany, with white silk drapings. There slept a handsome, young man.

Jack went over to a bureau beside the bed and saw five stones and a slingshot. "Five stones and a slingshot...could this be King David?"

Caleb pantomimed aiming a slingshot and said, "Do you mean *the* David who killed Goliath with one stone?" [4]

"How do you both know the same story?" asked Bill.
"The story is in the Old Testament, which both Jews and Catholics believe," said Jack.

Then, the man in the chamber rose and rang for his servants. "Quickly!" he said. "Today is the day we must gather the men of Judah to bring the Ark of God to our city!" David motioned to his servants to dress him quickly. Picturing the arrival of the Ark to his city, he smiled.

---

4 1 Sm 17:40–51.

Outside the palace stood a multitude of people anticipating the Ark's coming. Laughter and joy filled the people's hearts as they heard the trumpets sounding for its arrival. In haste, David ran to greet the Ark. From afar, he saw the priests surrounding it, a band of guards following closely, and musicians playing their hearts out. The crowd parted to make a path for the grand entrance. When he saw the Ark, David said, "How can the Ark of the Lord come to me?" [5] Later, he and his men escorted the Ark of the Lord to abide in the house of Obededom for three months, and the Lord blessed Obededom and all of his household. When David heard this, he brought the Ark back to his city and danced with all his might before the Lord.

The three astronauts watched King David lead the dance as cymbals, harps, and laughter resounded throughout the city, beckoning all to join in the joyful celebration.

Out of excitement, Caleb joined the dance and pulled his friends into the crowd. They danced until the music faded, and soon, they found themselves among vibrant roses growing in the recesses of a cave.

---

5 2 Sm 6:1–14.

CHAPTER 6

Mother of My Lord

OUTSIDE THE CAVE STOOD A modest, two-story adobe house. "I think we're in another time. Let's watch and see what happens next," Jack said.

Looking through an open window, they saw a maiden hurriedly packing items into a sash. She stepped outside and joined a young man preparing a donkey for a trip. The astronauts watched the man help her up onto the donkey, and together, they began their journey on a dusty path through the desert.

"I think we need to follow this couple and see where they're headed," said Jack.

"I can't believe we're seeing the Bible come alive!" said Caleb, still thinking of King David.

They followed the couple for two days. "Are you sure we're supposed to follow them?" asked Bill. "Where do you suppose they're going?"

"If we weren't supposed to travel with them, the Angel would have told us. I'm sure he's watching," said Jack.

"What's strange is that we haven't slept or eaten anything, but I don't feel tired or hungry at all," Bill noted. "How about you guys?"

"Yeah, it must have something to do with space and time travel," Jack said.

"Well, at least we don't have to worry about food," Bill added.

Jack and Bill noticed that Caleb had not said anything.

Caleb broke his silence and observed, "This man and this woman must be very holy. All they talk about is God."

"From what I can tell, they're Joseph and Mary, but I'm not positive," Jack said.

"This is the third day, and we still haven't gotten out of *this* scene," said Caleb.

Shortly, the man and woman came upon a house. The man walked the donkey to the far end of the house and tied it to a post.

The young Lady walked to the entrance of the house and called out, "Greetings, Cousin Elizabeth! It is Joseph and Mary."

A lady in her sixties with grey hair and a pregnant belly came to the doorway and greeted Mary. "And how does this happen to me that **the Mother of my Lord should come to me**? The moment your greeting reached my ears, the infant in my womb **leapt for joy**," [6] Elizabeth said as she took Mary's hand and placed it on her belly. They both felt the baby's feet dancing.

"It is Mary, the Mother of Jesus!" exclaimed Jack. "We're in the New Testament!"

Caleb went to touch Elizabeth's stomach to feel the baby move, but his hands went through her. However, he did see Elizabeth's stomach move, as if the baby was dancing inside of her.

Later, Joseph bid them farewell and told Mary that he would return in three months to escort her home once Elizabeth had her baby. Elizabeth and Zechariah's son would be named John.

When Joseph left Mary, the Angel brought the three astronauts out of history and back to the present.

The Angel said, "The home that Elizabeth lived in was once the home of Obededom."

"You mean the same home that David delivered the Ark to?" asked Jack.

"Yes," confirmed the Angel.

"So, where's the Ark now?" Caleb asked.

---

6 Lk 1:39–56.

"That is what you will also need to find out. I placed you in a scene with David in the Old Testament and a scene with Mary in the New Testament. Now, see if you can find the connection," the Angel said.

The three men were silent.

Jack spoke first, "David asked how it was that the **Ark** of the Lord came to him, and Elizabeth asked how it was that **Mary** would come to her."

"Good," the Angel said. "What do you see Bill?"

"Well, there's the number three," Bill pointed out.

Caleb questioned, "The number three?"

"I like numbers, so the number three caught my attention," Bill replied. "The **Ark** stayed three months in the house of Obededom, and **Mary** stayed for three months in the house of Elizabeth."

"That is correct. The Ark and Mary both stayed for three months. You found the connection. Caleb, did you find any connections between the stories?"

"I like to dance," Caleb said with excitement. "So, I noticed that David danced when he heard that the Ark blessed Obededom's house, and the baby in Elizabeth's womb 'leapt with joy' when it heard Mary's greetings."

"Each of you found a connection. This is an example of how stories foreshadow what will occur in the future. Do you see how the Old Testament foreshadows what will happen in the New Testament?"

"I see the connections, but how will this help us find the Ark?" Jack asked.

"Be patient. You need to uncover more clues before you can understand the mystery behind these connections," the Angel assured them. "It's a good start. There are more clues to investigate, and soon, the picture will be clear. I am giving you a Bible. See if you can use it as you solve more mysteries. It is an interactive Bible and can search for various topics."

Within an instant, the Angel left them, and they found themselves back in their shuttle.

"Okay, the Angel is gone. Let's see if we can contact Command Center. You two need to suit up and see if we can fix that satellite," Jack ordered. "Let's hurry before he comes back."

"What if the Angel is real, and fixing that satellite isn't going to stop the wars as he said? What if solving this mystery is the answer?" Caleb asked.

"I'm with Jack. We need to fix the satellite and get back to Earth. This might just be a space hallucination of some sort." Bill said.

"Okay, then we better do this quickly before the hallucination comes back," said Caleb.

"This is Jack. Come in, Command Center…" It was no use. Nothing on the shuttle was working. It was as if the shuttle was in sleep mode. The hatch wouldn't open.

"The Space Shuttle is still moving, right?" Bill said. "What orbit is the International Space Station in right now? I think there are other scientists on it. We can transmit a message through the radio receiver to the shuttle nearby."

The three astronauts worked on the radio receiver so that they could send radio waves.

"The message was sent, but I can't tell if it was received," Bill said.

"We'll have to wait and see if anyone responds," Jack said.

"In the meantime, let's continue solving this Ark of the Covenant mystery," Caleb said. "I think God wants us to help stop the war, and only He knows how to help us do that."

Bill didn't answer, but these events had rocked his atheistic view. Jack was trying to make sense of it all. He believed in God, but God hadn't been on his mind since college. Everything he learned in Catholic school was long forgotten.

The Bible was floating in the air in the space shuttle. It floated toward Jack and hit his head. He took it in his hand and began to flip through it.

"We might as well try to solve this Ark of the Covenant mystery if we want the Angel to get us back to Earth," Jack said.

Caleb and Bill both agreed. They read from the Old Testament first, searching for anything related to the Ark.

The grace which is given me in this hour will not be repeated in the next. It may be given me again, but it will not be the same grace. Time goes on, never to return again. Whatever is enclosed in it will never change; it seals with a seal for eternity.

— DIARY OF ST. FAUSTINA, #62

CHAPTER 7

Connection

HOURS LATER, THE ANGEL APPEARED to the astronauts. "Are you ready to delve into history again?" the Angel asked.

Bill pulled out their helmets to give to each of his crewmates. "I think these will help us move through time without headaches," he said.

The Angel smiled at his clever idea and told him that wouldn't be necessary.

They were immediately transported into the desert and saw a city on a hill enclosed in an impregnable brick wall, about twenty feet high. They saw thousands of soldiers processing around the city wall.

"Oh no! I think we're in the middle of a battle," Caleb said.

The Ark of the Covenant was at the front of the procession. They saw seven priests carrying ram's horns ahead of the Ark, ready to blow them. They watched as the Ark and the soldiers marched around the city.

"This scene reminds me of a song my mother would sing to me when I was a child," Jack said. "Maybe the Jews learned this too: 'Joshua fought the battle of Jericho, Jericho, Jericho, and the walls came tumblin' down, down, down…'"

As Jack finished singing, they heard the seven trumpets blare and an uproar of clamorous shouts. Crash! Boom! Bricks rumbled down the hillside as the wall surrounding the evil city crumbled to the ground. The soldiers ecstatically cheered as they clambered over the debris rushing into the city.

"Whoa, what kind of powerful song is that?" Bill asked.

"It wasn't the song. It was the Ark. It has power," Caleb interjected.

Just then, they were transported into another time in history.

"Wait! I need to put my helmet oooon!" shouted Bill, but it was too late. He hung onto his helmet as they raced through time. A huge wooden structure loomed a few feet in front of them. The three astronauts heard the banging of hammers and found an opening to enter. The bottom of the structure curved up on both sides and once inside they viewed a large, empty space like a barn. A wooden staircase positioned in the center revealed a second floor. Once on the second floor, the men found themselves outside, breathing in fresh air. Close by, an elderly man was directing three young men working on the structure.

"A woman emerged from the stairs carrying a jug of water, "Noah, boys, come take a rest."

"Noah's Ark? No way! I was wondering what this huge thing was doing in the middle of a desert," Bill exclaimed.

Caleb looked at Bill and said, "Wait... we thought you didn't know the Bible."

"I saw the movie 'Noah'."

"There are many inaccurate movies depicting stories on the Bible, but this is the real Noah's Ark," Caleb said. "Anyway, this is humongous! Way bigger than I imagined!"

Suddenly, music drifted in from afar. People were clapping and dancing while these men were pounding away on their woodwork.

One of the sons addressed Noah, "Father, are you certain that God wants you to build this Ark? Look around Father, we live in the desert, and it has never flooded here. We've always listened to you, but are you sure God wants us to do this?"

Another son said, "It would take days of heavy rain to lift this off the earth."

"Have faith, sons. God always has a great plan. What seems foolish to humans, God uses to confound the wise. God plans to flood the entire Earth, but we will be saved by the Ark,"[7] Noah responded.

Then the Angel pulled the astronauts back to the present.

"Seeing the wall of Jericho come down on its own was amazing!" Jack said. "Then to see Noah with his sons working on the Ark! Wow!"

---

7 Gen 7:23.

"We witnessed the power of the Ark of the Covenant in the Battle of Jericho," Caleb said. "I don't know if we can even call it a 'battle' since they didn't need to do much to win the city except trust in God."

Bill asked the Angel, "What gives the Ark such great power?"

"The Ark is overshadowed by the presence of God," the Angel responded. "Not only is it powerful, but nothing unclean can touch it without suffering God's wrath."

"What do you mean by 'overshadowed'?" Bill asked.

The Angel read from the Old Testament: Overshadow here is used to reference **the presence of God as a bright cloud of glory**. The cloud is the presence of God."[8]

"Angel Gabriel used similar words in the New Testament when he said to Mary, 'The Holy Spirit will come upon you, and the power of the Most High will overshadow you,'"[9] the Angel explained.

"How was Mary able to survive God's cloud of glory when others couldn't?" Jack asked.

"Because Mary is full of grace, meaning that she is without sin," the Angel said.

"'Full of grace' means that Mary is pure and holy," Caleb said. "So does that mean, God can only live in someone who is pure and holy?"

The Angel smiled. "Yes, you are piecing it together," he said. "Now, what did you learn about Noah's Ark?"

"Well, the two Arks don't look anything alike," Caleb answered. "However, Noah said that those in the Ark would be saved...like when the people took the Ark of the Covenant into battle."

"The stories of the Old Testament are telling us that the Ark of the Covenant is a powerful weapon in battle, and all those in the Ark are protected," the Angel said.

"You said that the symbols in the Old Testament take on life in the New Testament," Jack said. "We haven't seen it take on life."

---

8 Ex 40:34.

9 Lk 1:35.

"Well, now that you have enough information on the Ark, let's look again at the similarities you found between the Old and New Testament," the Angel said. He sketched a table for them as they listed what they learned.

The Ark of the Covenant[10]	
Old Testament	New Testament
1. David asked, "How can the Ark of the Lord come to me?"	1. Elizabeth asked, "How does this happen to me, that the Mother of my Lord should come to me?"
2. David danced with joy at seeing the Ark.	2. Elizabeth's baby leaped with joy upon hearing Mary's voice.
3. The Ark stayed for three months at the house of Obededom.	3. Mary stayed for three months at the house of Elizabeth.
4. The Ark cannot be touched or looked at by anyone who is unclean—meaning someone who is not pure and holy.	4. Mary is "full of grace," meaning that she is pure and holy.
5. The Ark was overshadowed by a cloud of glory, which is the presence of God.	5. Mary was overshadowed by the Holy Spirit.

Once the list was complete, Jack said, "The Ark of the Covenant is a symbol in the Old Testament; Mary is the living form of the Ark in the New Testament! So, Mary is the Ark of the Covenant?"

The Angel confirmed, "Yes, that is correct! God's great plan was to create the perfect human vessel to contain His Son, Jesus. Jesus chose to come to Earth through the womb of Mary. We are all destined for a purpose. Mary's purpose was to be the Mother of God. Now you see how the stories in the Old and New Testaments are connected.

---

10 See similar comparisons between the Old and New Testaments related to the Ark of the Covenant by Scott Hahn in his book, *Understanding the Scripture* 26.

You did well, but—not to quell your enthusiasm—we're not done yet. You need to solve the mystery of the three items you saw Moses place inside the Ark of the Covenant. They are the stone tablets, the manna, and the rod. God has hidden his most precious treasure in the Ark of the Covenant and it is waiting to be revealed. You have seen how important the stories are in the Bible. Read the Bible if you want to increase your knowledge of God. St. Jerome was correct to say, 'Ignorance of Scripture is ignorance of Christ.'"

The Angel left them to think about the three clues contained in the Ark. He went to update the Angels of the Cosmos on the status of the astronauts.

And the temple of God was opened in heaven: and the ark of his testament was seen in his temple, and there were lightnings, and voices, and an earthquake, and great hail.

— REVELATION 11:19

CHAPTER 8

Stone Tablets

CALEB STILL COULDN'T BELIEVE HOW he had been so misinformed about the New Testament as a child.

How can the Jews not have seen this truth for over two thousand years? he asked himself.

"Let me see that Bible," Caleb said as he grabbed the book from Jack. "So, the Old Testament contains symbols that come to life in the New Testament?"

"To tell you the truth, I don't remember learning any of these connections in my twelve years of Catholic schooling," replied Jack.

"This is all new to me, too," Bill said "and I still don't know why God just didn't state that in the Bible for y'all. But I get it now. It's like buildin' a skyscraper. You first need a blueprint—a plan—which is what God had in the Old Testament. Then, the plan is put into action, creatin' the skyscraper, which is the fulfillment in the New Testament."

Jack said, "I've heard that Mary is the Ark of the Covenant, but I never understood what that meant until now."

"All right, so now we know that Mary is the Ark, but what does that have to do with helping us stop the war or getting us home?" Caleb asked.

"This is all interesting, but what the Angel needs to do is give us a weapon to defend ourselves from our enemies," Bill said.

"As the Angel said, God doesn't work that way. Let's investigate the three items in the Ark. The stone tablets, the manna, and the rod," said Jack.

"The stone tablets contain the Ten Commandments," Caleb said.

"Can you show me where that is in the Bible?" Bill said.

Caleb searched the Book of Exodus. Just as he pointed to the section, they were taken back in time. They found themselves on the peak of Mount Sinai and there they saw Moses, his face illuminated under the cloud of glory. A light more radiant than the sun veiled by a white cloud let loose a single beam of such considerable intensity, it left the surrounding region with an indelible mark of God's presence. They witnessed a hand stretch down from Heaven and a finger inscribe the Ten Commandments on two stone tablets.[11]

---

11 Ex 31:18; 32:15–16.

"Can you believe this? This is God writing His commandments on the stones with His finger," Caleb exclaimed in awe.

Moses prostrated himself in thanksgiving to God for His Eternal Laws. God told Moses to go down the mountain and rebuke the people because they had offended Him by making their own god out of a molten calf. Moses picked up the stone tablets and went down the mountain. When he saw the people dancing and worshiping the golden calf, he grew angry and threw down the tablets, smashing them into pieces.

Tears ran down Caleb's face, seeing the idolatry among the people. He rushed to the broken stone tablets and tried to put the precious pieces back together, but they slipped through his fingers.

The Angel brought the astronauts back to the present. "I am glad that you found the right section of the Bible for the stone tablets. Why do you think these Commandments are so important?"

"They are the tools God gave man to help him reach Heaven," Jack responded.

"Yes, and the Ten Commandments are eternal and cannot be changed," said the Angel. "God gave them to man to protect them, but man has rejected God's Words and His protection. His laws can help man separate truth from falsehood, good from evil, and right from wrong. If you take away His laws, you take away the guide to truth. The God of Abraham, Isaac, and Jacob is the only God who has ever given mankind laws to lead them to Heaven."[12]

"You mean no other god has ever come down to guide man in this way?" asked Bill.

"There is only one God, and it is the God of Abraham, Isaac, and Jacob," stated the Angel. "Words have power, but God's words have supernatural power. In John's gospel, He wrote that Jesus is the Word, and 'the Word was God … and the Word became flesh and made His dwelling among us.'[13] God's Word takes on life, and Jesus is the Word of the Father in human form."

---

12 Deut 4:7–8.

13 Jn 1:1, 14.

Caleb repeated, "Jesus is the Word of the Father in human form."

"That's correct. The Word was made flesh—that is, the Living Word, Jesus, took the form of a human," the Angel repeated.

"Didn't He know that taking a human form would make Him vulnerable to pain and suffering?" Bill asked.

"Yes, He knew," said the Angel.

"But...God can't die, right?" asked Bill.

"No, God cannot die, but He can if He takes human form. In this way, Jesus was able to offer His life for the world."

"Jesus offered His life to fulfill His Father's plan, even to suffer the death of crucifixion?" Caleb was moved by the thought of His suffering.

"Yes, if humans knew how much God loves them, they would die of joy," the Angel responded.

As they were talking, they heard the blast of the second trumpet.

"What was that?" Jack asked.

"It is the second trumpet," the Angel said.

"Wait, what trumpet?" asked Jack.

"The trumpets are God's warnings to mankind signifying an impending catastrophe to the world due to the consequences of sin," said the Angel.

"*Trumpets?* How many trumpets are there? Does that mean the end of the world is coming?" Jack asked.

"There are seven trumpets, and two have already sounded," the Angel said. "The seventh trumpet will sound the end of man's time on Earth and marks the beginning of a new era of peace."

"The end of time? What will happen on Earth when the final trumpet sounds?" asked Caleb.

"As each trumpet sounds, Earth progresses toward a terrible tribulation and it will seem like Satan is in control. However, when the final trumpet sounds, God will destroy Satan and reclaim His dominion over a new Earth," said the Angel.

"It's reassuring that God hasn't given up on us," Caleb said with hope.

CHAPTER 9

The Father's Children

Before I formed form you in the womb, I knew you;
before you were born, I dedicated you.

—JEREMIAH 1:5

THERE WAS A GREAT RUMBLING across the galaxy after the second trumpet sounded.

The Angel turned to the astronauts and said, "Come, follow me." As he opened a portal, they heard the laughter of children. What they saw was a sea of children surrounded by Angels.

"There must be thousands of children here. What is this place?" Bill asked.

"There are millions of children here," the Angel corrected. "This place of limbo is where aborted children go."

"Aborted children?" Bill swallowed, his brow creased with concern.

"More babies have been aborted than all the dead combined from all the wars on Earth," responded the Angel.

"Why are they here?" asked Jack.

The Angel said, "Although these children have been killed in the body, their souls live eternally."

An Angel with fiery red hair approached them and said, "God's mercy permits these children to be here because they have not committed any personal sins, and therefore, do not deserve to be in Hell. These children were deprived of a chance for life and for the opportunity to take their seat in heaven. They were torn apart and cut up alive during an abortion. They have suffered a great evil from the hands of man. Here, God will comfort them, and He will bring justice to their suffering."

Then he quoted from Isaiah: "'The fruit of the womb they shall not spare, nor shall they have eyes of pity for children.'14 Satan does not want mankind to inherit the empty thrones that would have been for his fallen Angels had they followed God. Out of anger against God, Satan and his cohorts have gone after mankind, deceiving them even into death out of anger against God."

The Angel with red hair waved his right hand and an hourglass appeared. He said, "Even the demons work for a common goal: to destroy humans. They know they are running out of time. They are aware that once the thrones are filled, God will come with His wrath against them for the sins they have committed against Him, namely the depopulation of humanity. Satan gave humans the tool of abortion to achieve his goals. Sadly, Satan has succeeded; thousands of children are being aborted every day. Humans are blinded by the generational effects of disregarding natural law and do not realize that they are working with Satan to achieve their own destruction. Soon, time will run out, and procreation will cease."

Some of the children came over and spoke to the men. "Earth will experience the wrath of God due to the blood of abortion. Stop abortion, and you can stop the coming war. If man does not stop abortion, the world will suffer from disease, natural disasters, and much more."

The Angel turned to the astronauts and said, "You have seen and heard from the children. Your mission is to help others on Earth see the truth." He brought the men back to their space shuttle.

After a few moments of deliberation, Bill said, "I always believed in the theory of evolution, and that we're all organisms that will eventually die, and that the end would be the end. At exactly what moment does life begin?

---

14 Isaiah 13:18.

The Angel explained, "Life begins at conception; without the moment of conception, there would be no life, no beginning."

Bill said, "Wow... that makes much more sense than all the theories scientists have come up with." The Angel left the men to think more about what they had been shown.

"I want to understand more about the soul. Let's ask this interactive Bible to find anything related to 'spirit' and 'soul' and see what it says," Caleb said. The Bible displayed many verses.

Caleb said, "Here, this is from Ecclesiastes 12:7: 'And the dust returned to the Earth as it once was, and the life breath returns to God who gave it.'"

"Why does it say that we were once dust even before we die?" Bill asked.

"Because Adam was made from clay, which is dirt, and if we come from Adam, then after we die, we return to Earth as dirt or dust," explained Caleb.

"And the breath of life is the soul that God gave the body, and it returns to God when we die," Jack stated.

"Here is another one from Matthew 10:28: 'And do not be afraid of those who kill the body but cannot kill the soul; rather, be afraid of the one who can destroy both the body and soul in Gehenna,'" Jack read.

"What's Gehenna?" Bill asked.

"It's Hell," Jack answered.

Bill took the Bible and said, "So, the soul either returns to God in Heaven or ends up in Hell without God."

The men discussed the soul at length. As they read about the raising of Lazarus, they were transported to the tomb where he laid. He was wrapped from head to toe in white linen. The cave reeked of rotting flesh, for it had been four days since Lazarus' death.

A voice from outside said, "Lazarus, come out!"

The astronauts witnessed as Lazarus came back to life, the smell of death immediately left the cave. Lazarus peeled back the linen from his face, rose, and walked out of the cave into the sunlight. The three men looked on in astonishment.

"How does a dead man come back to life?" Bill asked.

"And who called Lazarus?" asked Caleb.

"It's Jesus who called him. Jesus' words have power over life and Lazarus' resurrection demonstrated His power. This story of Lazarus is important in the Bible because it foreshadows Jesus' death and resurrection." Jack was surprised that he still remembered some of the stories of the Bible.

"Jesus does have power over life and death," Caleb said in shock.

"Did Buddha or Mohammed or other gods resurrect as Jesus did?" Bill asked.

"No, only Jesus resurrected, as witnessed by His followers. Also, neither Buddha nor Mohammed ever claimed that they were god in any way," said Jack.

> *Then God said, "Let us[15] make man in our image, after our likeness. [...] The Lord God formed man out of the clay of the ground and blew into his nostrils the breath of life, and so man became a living being."*
>
> — GENESIS 1:26 AND 2:7

---

15 God the Father uses "us" to refer to Jesus, His Son and to the Holy Spirit—three Persons in One God.

CHAPTER 10

Second Trumpet

THE SECOND GUARDIAN OF THE Trumpet took his place atop the West
Gate of the City of God. He extended his hands in front of him and out
of his mouth came a loud vibration. He faced his open mouth in the
direction of the oncoming meteorites to direct them away from Earth.
The sound waves propelled the meteorites several light-years away, avert-
ing a devastating calamity. The sins of man have given Satan power over
the cosmos to attack the Earth. Then the Guardian blasted a wakeup
call to the universe, penetrating the stillness with his deep, thunderous
voice, and said, "As it is written in the Book of Daniel 'from the time that
the daily sacrifice[16] is abolished and the horrible abomination[17] is set up,
there shall be one-thousand two-hundred and ninety days. Blessed is the
man who has patience and perseveres until the last of the one-thousand
three-hundred and thirty-five days.'"[18]

The Angels of the Cosmos not only guarded space and the planets
but also oversaw the most important planet: Earth. They were grateful
for the Guardian's help in diverting the meteorites. They had enough
work in holding off the earthquakes, floods, and natural disasters,

---

16 The daily sacrifice is the Holy Sacrifice of the Mass.

17 The horrible abomination is also known as the "Abomination of Desolation." See also
Matthew 24:15–21 and Mark 13:14–19. The Abomination of Desolation is the elimi-nation of the
Most Holy Eucharist, the Most Precious Body and Blood of Our Lord, Jesus Christ, from the
Holy Mass and Holy Tabernacles. It is the invalid consecration by a priest whereby the bread and
wine are not transformed into Our Lord, Jesus Christ.

18 Dn 12:11–12.

which constantly threatened to destroy mankind. Soon they would not be able to prevent the oncoming obliteration of a third of the Earth which would be swallowed up and engulfed in water and then fire. A far more fearful punishment would have awaited the people of Earth if it were not for the few faithful, whose prayers lessened the extent of their retribution.

The Angel of Pure Contemplation was heading back to the Throne of God when the Angels of the Cosmos came to ask him about Earth's situation. He explained, "The Second Trumpet sounded because Earth's high court is not upholding the Eternal and Natural Laws and immorality on Earth is worse than at the time of Sodom and Gomorrah. The children of Earth are willingly chaining themselves to Satan. They are exchanging their freedom for slavery," he explained somberly.

The Angel of the Cosmos pitied the people of Earth. He responded, "Jesus gave the people of Earth seven great means to destroy the chain that binds them to Satan."

"Yes, but by their own hands, they are closing these seven means to attain freedom from Satan." As he said this, he raised his hands and a portal opened. The Angel of Pure Contemplation said, "God has sent me to witness what is happening on Earth as well as in the depths of the Earth. See what Lucifer, the cunning snake, is teaching his cohorts."

A second Angel followed, saying: "Fallen, fallen is Babylon the great, that made all the nations drink the wine of her licentious passion."

— REVELATION 14:8

CHAPTER 11
The Fiery Pit

IN THE VERY DEPTHS OF Earth's molten core, in the recesses of a cavern ablaze with scorching flames, stood a throne formed from the Earth's ashes. Satan sat, exalted on his throne as he looked down the many steps separating him from his foul minions. He looked disgusted as he shook his head, murmuring under his breath, "They are so stupid. They can't even think for themselves without me. Don't they understand anything?" Then he stood up and settled the commotion as they discussed if tempting the humans to sin enough.

Satan shouted, "Stop the bickering! Are you all related to Wormwood?[19] Do I have to spell everything out to you for you to understand? No, tempting those idiots on Earth isn't enough! You must water down and eliminate any access to the seven means He instituted for them to escape our clutches. They can commit all the sins on Earth, but if they make use of the Confessional, all of those sins will be forgiven, and they will be absolved. Aren't you tired of tempting them 24/7 and then having all that effort go to waste in *one moment* by absolution? Well, if you destroy the credibility of the priest and the Catholic Church, who will go to Confession at all? We must attack the priests and kill them! Leave the unholy ones alone; they already work for us; but help each other by multiplying your temptations on holy priests. Remember, no priest, no Mass, and no Eucharist. See, the only reason the Catholic Church is still standing is that the Eucharist lives there. *He* lives there.

---

19 *Wormwood is a character in the book: The Screwtape Letters by C.S. Lewis.*

Otherwise, the Church He created would have been destroyed," he said with disdain as the thought of God humiliating himself for those useless creatures disgusted him.

One of the minions said, "But, all it takes is for them to commit one mortal sin, and their souls belong to us. What have we to fear?"

"Their access to Confession. Don't you get it?" Satan said.

"Why don't we kill all those who have mortal sins so that they won't access confession?"

"God is protecting them by giving them time to repent. Also, we must fight against people's Guardian Angels. Why else haven't these humans all gone to hell yet? Have you seen how sinful they are? He is too merciful!" Satan responded.

Then another minion asked, "Can you list the seven means that these souls can escape from our clutches?"

"I am listing them. Aren't you listening?" Satan said with irritation, throwing down his scepter. This is the reason I leave the teachings to Screwtape.[20] He is much more patient with you dummies."

"Fine, the first is Baptism. You should know this one. Original sin is taken away and they are made a child of God, which means they can steal your throne in Heaven. Second, is Reconciliation or Confession. This is a dangerous one, since they can access this often." He smirked, "Luckily not many of them do. We have a team at the top which has gone after the Sacrament of Confession. We may not win the battle on this, but we must try to eliminate it by wearing them down. Third, is Holy Communion. This one should be easy; many don't believe in the Real Presence of Him in the Bread and Wine and so many commit even more sin by receiving Him unworthily. We have seen the increase in disre-spect for Holy Communion through the years which is a positive sign in the right direction. Fourth, is Confirmation. This Sacrament places the Holy Spirit in their souls to help them fight for their faith. We've done a fine job in this area by keeping the kids distracted with video games and destroying their innocence by teaching them about sex at an early

---

20 Screwtape is a character in the book: *The Screwtape Letters* by C.S. Lewis

age. By the time they are in High School, they won't even believe God exists. Fifth, is the Sacrament of Marriage. We have finally reached over fifty percent of marriages ending in divorce. Immediately the demons erupted in applauses. We are redefining marriage and causing confusion defining sexual identity. The family structure is crumbling, and it will not be long before it's demolished. They are so gullible and easily manipulated. They will believe anything now and when He comes to Earth again, He will hardly find any more faithful. The fifth is the Priesthood. This one has been a sore in my eyes to see those unworthy humans as priests of Christ. Finally, there is the Anointing of the Sick. We are close to our goal here with many places legalizing euthanasia. We want them to die as soon as possible so that they do not unite their sufferings with Him. They don't understand the value of suffering, especially before death. Their sufferings if united to Him can help reduce their time in purgatory and even save souls. It is good that this is not known by many. We must ensure that they do not have access to the other Sacraments before death. But if they somehow die a repentant death before being euthanized, then at least they will suffer longer in purgatory before going to Heaven. We can at least have that satisfaction."

Satan scanned the pit and saw for the first time that they were all listening. "I see that you finally understand that tempting these souls on Earth is not the end goal. It is the means to enslave them to us. We can never let our guard down because of these deadly 'Seven Sacraments' of the Catholic Church."

The Angels of Pure Contemplation closed the portal and said, "People are not even aware of what they are up against."

"However, God has given each soul a Guardian Angel to help fend off these devils who keep tempting them with evil and distracting them from God," said the Angel of the Cosmos. The Angel of Pure Contemplation agreed, and he flew away to meet with God. The Angels of the Cosmos went to see St. Michael and said, "We need more prayers from the children of Earth to gain the upper hand over darkness. Satan has discovered many ways to prevent these souls from getting to Heaven."

St. Michael responded, "I will continue to ask for more prayers from the faithful. Are the sun, moon, and stars ready for the Great Warning?"

"The sun and moon are ready," the Angels of the Cosmos replied. "The stars are still being formed by the astronauts. Once the astronauts comprehend the mystery of the Ark of the Covenant, they will be able to carry out their mission. With greater knowledge and with the grace they earn, they will help open the eyes of many."

CHAPTER 12

Ripple

SEEING THE THOUSANDS OF CHILDREN in the portal brought back horrible memories of war for Bill. He recalled his tour of duty in the Middle East.

It was high noon that day, and the blazing sun was beating down on his tan camouflage uniform, gluing the sweaty clothing to his back.

Bill thought, *one more tour in Afghanistan, and I get to go home to Linda.*

He and his battalion were searching a compound for terrorists—the last compound on their list. As they turned the corner, Bill spotted the reflection of light shining from one of the mud houses that constituted most Afghanistan homes. He raised his right hand, signaling the men to stop. No one moved. He motioned to one of his men to pick up a tin can at his feet and toss it in the direction of the light.

As he tossed it, a shot went out. Bullets spewed from several machine guns positioned on the building's roof across from where they were positioned. Bill and his men took cover under the doorways of evacuated buildings, and he ordered his M1 tank to fire away. The tank released a laser-guided missile that pummeled into the house, toppling the building onto the unsuspecting enemy.

Bill and his men enclosed the area, and upon entering, they found that innocent women and children had been crushed along with the enemy. The enemy had used the women and children as shields as they shot at the American soldiers. There were no survivors.

War, what is all this for? Bill thought.

Since that time, he wondered, *Who was the real enemy, and what was his strategy? If it wasn't for Linda, this world wouldn't be worth living in.* He thought of how he responded to the news Linda gave him a few weeks before he left for this space mission. *I was so wrong, but it's too late now to tell her.* He paused for a moment and prayed for the first time. *God, if you exist, I'm sorry.*

"Bill, you okay?" Caleb asked. "You've been quiet since we got back to the space shuttle."

Caleb's voice brought Bill back to the present. "I just had an intense flashback ...just trying to make sense of what is happening."

"I know what you mean. I was taught not to believe in or read the New Testament," Caleb said.

Jack was at the other end of the shuttle, grappling with the fact that he had abandoned God and lost sight of the higher purpose of life. He took out a rosary from his pocket and touched the worn, wooden beads as he reminisced about his mother.

He recalled a little eight-year-old boy who would go to Church with his mother at night to visit Jesus in the chapel. One night, they were sitting in front of a wooden chest coated in gold. Two Angels knelt on top of the chest, facing each other with their heads bowed. It was a small replica of the Ark of the Covenant. When his mother finished praying the Rosary, the boy took off his shoes and stood up.

"Son, what are you doing?" his mother asked.

He whispered, "I'm doing what Moses did before he entered Holy ground."

Curious as to what her son would do next, his mother gave him a nod to continue. He walked barefoot to the box and knelt in front of it, bowed his head to the floor, and prayed.

"My God, I believe, I adore, I trust, and I love You! I ask pardon of You for those who do not believe, do not trust, do not hope, and do not love You!" [21]

His mother joined him, and they repeated the prayer three times.

---

21 *Her Own Words to the Nuclear Age: The Memoirs of Sr. Lucia* by John Haffert, pp. 8 and 245.

As they were leaving the Church, the boy asked his mother, "Can Jesus see me through the tabernacle?"

She said, "Yes, He can."

"Can He see through lead?" he asked.

"Oh, yes. He can see through lead and even through the hearts of men," she replied.

"Can He fly?" he quickly added with wide eyes, wondering if God was like Superman.

"I'll have to read to you the story about the Ascension of Jesus when all of His disciples witnessed Him going up to Heaven," she responded.

"That's so cool!" The little boy smiled as he leaned into his mother's side and hugged her. Then he asked, "Mom, why are we visiting the Church so much lately?"

"Well, many evil things are happening in the world, and one day, people might not be able to attend Mass at Church anymore. So, we should seek God here in the Blessed Sacrament and at Mass while we can still find Him. More and more people do not believe in God, and they blame Him for all of the wars and disasters that are going on."

"Why doesn't God stop the wars and disasters?" he asked. "He has great power, doesn't He?"

"That's a good question, but wars and disasters are caused by humans. God always has a good reason for not interfering. Nothing bad comes from God. Our every word, thought, and deed influence the entire universe. If we could understand this, we would not blame God but rather look at ourselves," she explained.

"How can our actions influence the universe?" he asked.

"Imagine what happens when you throw a little stone into a pond. The stone causes a rippling effect on the water. It's the same with each person's actions. There is no such thing as a private sin or a sin that does not hurt anyone. No thought, word, or deed goes unnoticed by God. Sin causes the loss of grace for the sinner, the Church, and all of humanity. We all lose when we sin."

Coming back to the present, Jack realized that his mother knew the Church would be persecuted in the future and that the world would come to a disastrous end if it did not turn back to God.

The three astronauts fell asleep, each with their thoughts on God. The Angel entered Caleb's dream, escorting him back to his childhood. It was when he was twelve, during the Passover Feast: the time when he stopped waiting for the coming of the Messiah. Every year, he and his family would follow the Jewish tradition of celebrating Passover with special foods. They sang traditional songs and recounted the story of their ancestors' flight from Egypt. This year, it was his turn to go to the door and see if the Messiah had come. He went to the door to open it, but in his heart, he knew no one would be there. But he got up and did it anyway. He slowly opened the door, and there he saw a man illuminated in lights. He stretched out his hands to Caleb. Caleb's heart began to pound, and he reached for the man's hands. As he stretched out his hands, the figure disappeared.

Caleb shouted, "No!" He woke up from his dream.

That was so real. I saw the Messiah. He did come…

Caleb grabbed the Bible and broke it open and absorbed the words of his Messiah. He spent the night reading and learning the Messiah's teachings about love; love of God, and love of each other—to love your enemy and to turn the other cheek. He read about the many miracles God performed: healing the sick, giving sight to the blind, curing the lepers, raising the dead, releasing those possessed by demons, and multiplying food.

Caleb questioned, *This is the man —no— this is the God, that so many wanted to kill and even today hate His teachings. Why?*

He reflected on his own people and saw how stubborn the Jews had been from the time of the Old Testament to the present. He thought of the many times they had abandoned God and yet, God was still with them.

Oh, how blind we are, Caleb thought.

Caleb reached the passage where the Messiah was falsely accused and sentenced to a criminal's death by crucifixion. He imagined his own hands and feet nailed to the cross. His heart wrenched with pain, his breathing became difficult, and tears welled in his eyes.

He whispered to himself, *We have a God willing to suffer and die for us, for me. What god would do this? What God would love us like this?*

CHAPTER 13

Manna

THE NEXT MORNING, JACK WENT over to see Caleb. He noticed Caleb's tired face and said, "Why are your eyes red? Rough night?"

"No, it was the best sleepless night I've ever had," responded Caleb.

"Do you need to rest some before we start solving the mystery?" said Jack.

"No! I want to get started. There's more to the Bible than I've ever imagined. I found manna in the Old Testament and I bet it's there in the New Testament," said Caleb.

"What does manna mean in the Old Testament?"

"It was the bread that came down from Heaven to feed the Israelites in the desert when they ran out of food," Caleb explained.

"I see. Jesus is called the 'Bread of Life' in the New Testament Gospel of John."

"They must be connected," Bill chimed in.

After reading and discussing John's gospel, the Angel appeared to them.

"We examined some of the clues involving the manna," Jack said to the Angel. "There are so many stories, so we chose just a few to go over with you."

"Wonderful!" The Angel was happy to see that they were using the Bible. "Share with me what you found."

"The word 'manna' was first used in the story of Moses," Caleb explained. "God called Moses to lead the people of Israel out of Egypt to escape the oppression of King Pharaoh. They escaped from Pharaoh and lived in the wilderness for 40 days. But they began to complain to Moses when they ran out of food."[22]

Caleb read, "'Then the Lord said to Moses, 'I will rain down bread from Heaven for you... On seeing it, the Israelites asked one another, 'What is this?' for they did not know what it was. But Moses told them, 'This is the bread, which the Lord has given you to eat.' From then on, they called the bread 'manna,' meaning 'What is this?'"[23]

The Angel asked, "What else did you learn about the manna?"

"God commanded Moses to fill a golden bowl with manna and place it in the Ark to remind the people that God fed and sustained them in the wilderness after they escaped from Egypt,"[24] Bill said.

"What about references to manna or bread in the New Testament?" the Angel asked.

Jack said, "There are many, but first, would you please take us back in time to the New Testament, in the Gospel of John, chapter six, beginning with verse twenty-two?"

The astronauts were then transported through time. When they stopped moving through the whirlwind, they saw a massive crowd of people running through the sand to the sea. They were scanning the surroundings in search of something. Realizing that what they were

---

22 Ex 16:2–3.

23 Ex 16:4, 15–31.

24 Ex 16:32–34.

looking for was not there, hundreds rushed to get into the many small boats lined along the shore.

Someone on the shoreline said, "He is not here, we think He has gone to Capernaum." So, all the boats turned around and followed the other boats out to Capernaum. The people looked hungry but joyful and hopeful.

The three astronauts hopped onto one of the boats heading to Capernaum.

A man shouted, "There he is! Over there!"

Once the crowd came to Capernaum, they quickly got out and rushed to the man walking along the shoreline. They said to him, "Rabbi, when did you get here?"[25]

The Rabbi responded, "Amen, amen, I say to you, you are looking for me not because you saw signs but because you ate the loaves and were filled. Do not work for food that perishes but for food that endures for eternal life, which the Son of Man will give you. For on Him the Father, God has set His seal."[26]

The people said to him, "What can we do to accomplish the works of God?"[27]

He answered, "This is the work of God, that you believe in the one He sent."[28]

Then, they asked him for a sign that they could believe. They said, "Our ancestors ate manna in the desert, as it is written: 'He gave them bread from Heaven to eat.'"[29]

The Rabbi, who was Jesus, told them of the bread of life, which comes from His Father. "Your ancestors ate manna in the desert, but they died [...]. **I am the living bread** that came down from Heaven; whoever eats this bread will live forever; and **the bread that I will give is my flesh** for the life of the world."[30]

---

25 Jn 6:25.
26 Jn 6:26–27.
27 Jn 6:28.
28 Jn 6:29.
29 Jn 6:31.
30 Jn 6:49–51.

The crowd began to murmur against Jesus and quarreled among themselves. Some argued that Jesus meant that the bread was a symbol of Him—not that He meant to eat His Flesh. They argued, "How can this man give us [His] flesh to eat?"[31]

Jesus clarified that He did not mean it as a symbol and repeated what He said: "Amen, amen, I say to you, unless you eat the flesh of the Son of Man and drink His blood, you will not have life within you. Whoever eats my flesh and drinks my blood has eternal life, and I will raise him on the last day."[32]

"Look," Jack said, "the people are getting back into their boats. They don't understand how Jesus can be the Living Bread."

Caleb saw how the people desperately wanted to believe that he was the Messiah. They have been seeking Him all morning and afternoon, but because they had a preconceived idea of how God would come to them, they couldn't believe the truth before them. He began to believe that Jesus is the Bread of life and shouted, "Hey, come back! He's not talking about cannibalism. He's God and can change bread into Himself!"

"What are you doing? They can't hear you," Bill said to Caleb.

"What? It doesn't hurt to try," Caleb shrugged.

The Angel transported them back to the present.

"Wow! It was amazing to see Jesus and to hear His voice and His words!" they proclaimed.

"The people were so blessed to have Jesus with them in their lifetime, and it's so unfortunate that they didn't believe...that I didn't believe," Caleb said.

"You know," Bill said, "just seeing the looks on those people's faces, I saw that they wanted to follow Jesus. But the idea of eating His flesh and drinking His blood *is* hard to believe. I can understand why many of His disciples left Him upon hearing this. I would have thought He was crazy, too. They would never have thought that God would turn bread into Himself."

---

31 Jn 6:52.

32 Jn 6:53–54.

The Angel asked Jack, "Do you believe that this 'bread' Jesus is talking about is His flesh?"

"Yes, I remember reading in Genesis: God said, 'Let there be light,'[33] and there was light. Just by His words alone, He created the world, the animals, trees, and everything on Earth. God can do anything."

"There are many other examples in the Bible, such as water turning into blood or wine,[34]" Caleb added. "Remember when the Red Sea parted at Moses' command? If Moses can do that, then Jesus can turn bread into His flesh."

"With God, nothing is impossible," the Angel said. "Now that your faith has grown, you can understand this miracle."

Jack agreed. "My mother once said that belief is necessary for miracles to happen. When the people asked, 'What can we do to accomplish the works of God?' Jesus said, 'This is the work of God, that you believe in the one He sent.'[35] Jesus is saying that they can help Him accomplish His work by believing in what He says and obeying His command."

"Unfortunately," the Angel said, "even today, Christians do not believe and do not listen to Jesus. If believers and nonbelievers would visit Him in the Blessed Sacrament, He would give them the grace to believe. The Holy Eucharist is the greatest test of faith."

"Yeah, no kidding," Bill agreed, still taking it all in.

As they were about to go over the next clue, they heard the third trumpet. Heaven shook, and all stood still and waited.

Jesus then said to the Twelve, "Do you also want to leave?" Simon Peter answered him, "Master, to whom shall we go? You have the words of eternal life."

— John 6:67–68

---

33 Gen 1:3.
34 Ex 7:20; Jn 2:1–11.
35 Jn 6:28–29.

CHAPTER 14
The Father's Weapon

ANGELS STOOD IN LINE, EACH waiting for the Lady to assign them a scroll before being sent to Earth. Each scroll contained the name and location of a child of God. Earth is in time, and the Lady knew that time would soon run out. Two Angels accompanied the Lady, the Queen of Heaven and Earth. As each child is conceived in their mothers' womb, the Lady assigned them a Guardian Angel to guide and protect them through life on their journey to their eternal home in Heaven.

She prays that the mothers will allow their children to be born and that one day they would be united with their Father in Heaven for all eternity. When a child is conceived, it is given soul and flesh. The woman's womb is the vessel through which God has chosen to bring humanity into the world. It has been this way since the time of Adam and Eve. Never in the history of mankind has the vessel for procreation been attacked as it is currently. The Lady was battling against Satan, who would stop at nothing to prevent these children from being born.

Saint Michael the Archangel, informed the Queen, that her Father summoned her to the Grand Palace. As he was waiting for the Queen, Saint Michael recalled the First Battle, when Lucifer, now called Satan, had cleverly won over one-third of the Angels to fight against God Almighty. When Lucifer fell, one-third of God's thrones prepared for the Angels in Heaven were left empty. God filled these thrones with chosen souls who persevere in the faith to the end. From then on, Satan endeavored to stop man from seizing the empty thrones. He continuously contrives numerous, abominable ways to prevent souls from entering Heaven. Abortion, contraception, and the dissolution of marriage, just to name a few.

Once the Lady was finished handing out the scrolls for the day, Saint Michael updated her on the empty throne's status.

"My Lady," he said, "The empty thrones are filling up as Christians are martyred on Earth. Although only the Father knows the time and hour when he will bring his Kingdom to completion, the filling of the empty thrones shows us that the pre-Tribulation time is here.

The Queen nodded in agreement and quickly left for the Grand Palace to see her Father.

"My Daughter, I have used my power to forge a great weapon for mankind —an indestructible weapon that will save my people from their perversity," her Father began. "This weapon has been forged using the gold from the Ark of the Covenant and the five stones David used to take down Goliath." The Father presented a glimmering sword to his daughter. As she received it, the sword transformed into a beaded chain.

The Father held her hands and said, "This chain of the Rosary has been resharpened[36] throughout history and is now in its most powerful form. This weapon against evil must be in the hands of my faithful children on Earth. The only weapon greater than this is the Presence of Jesus in the Most Blessed Sacrament. Go, remind them that I gave them this weapon to use against the power of darkness and evil spirits."

The Lady took the Rosary and said, "Father, your goodness is abundant, and your love for your children is bountiful. I will hasten to remind

---

36 *Champions of the Rosary,* by Donald H. Calloway, MIC.

them and will plead with them to use this weapon as a sign of your love and protection."

I am the Lord and there is no other, there is no God besides me. It is I who arm you, though you know me not, so that toward the rising and the setting of the sun men may know that there is none besides me.

— Isaiah 45: 5–6

CHAPTER 1 5

Third Trumpet

As His natural order began to crumble, God commanded the third trumpet to sound. Inside the space shuttle, the astronauts were gathered at the table to talk about life at home. As they were speaking, a radiant figure appeared before them. He was tall, young, and handsome, with brown eyes and hair, wearing a carpenter's apron. They recognized him as the man who accompanied Mary to visit St. Elizabeth.

He greeted them and said, "I am Joseph, spouse of Mary and the foster-father of Jesus. I am here to let you know what is happening now and what will be happening on Earth. Satan is becoming bold as his followers on Earth visibly bring him into the world with their evil deeds. He will soon gain full power over Earth. If God does not interfere, the whole universe will collapse because of man's continued cooperation with the father of lies. Already as of now, earthquakes, fires and floods ravage the Earth. Leaving many people fearful of these uncertain times."

The astronauts looked at each other in shock, trying to digest St. Joseph's words. Jack asked, "What about our mission?"

Bill asked, "And our families? Are they still alive?"

"Do not be afraid. Your families are safe. There is still time for you to complete your mission and to go back and prepare your families and the world for what is to come." The astronauts listened attentively as St. Joseph outlined the events of the apocalypse.

A third Angel followed them and said in a loud voice, "Anyone who worships the beast or its image or accepts its mark on forehead or hand, will also drink the wine of God's fury, poured full strength into the cup of his wrath and will be tormented in burning sulfur before the holy Angels and before the lamb. The smoke of the fire that torments them will rise forever and ever, and there will be no relief day or night for those who worship the beast or its image or accept the Mark of its name."

— REVELATION 14: 9–11

CHAPTER 16

The Rod

BILL SAT STARING OUT IN space. His voice had a somber tone, "Looking from here, it seems so obvious now that there is someone behind all this. The world is like a puzzle that God left for us to put together to find Him. Just like how God uses numbers in the Bible to help us connect events. I never saw it, but you did." he said, looking at Caleb. "I'm sure there are other numbers and clues He left behind for us to study."

Caleb could sense the change in Bill and smiled.

Bill continued, "We use mathematical equations to explain many things in science, but these equations were left for us to unveil what has always been there. Neither the big bang theory nor the theory of evolution created mathematical equations; they didn't create intelligence. The real creator—the mathematician from the beginning—is God. He left these equations in His creation for us to find, to discover, and to comprehend what He has created."

Thoughts of the aborted children in the portal came back to Bill. He asked, "How do the male sperm and a female egg know how to form a human being? I mean, how do all the different body parts know how to work the way they do? How about the brain and its intelligence, or the beating heart and, well...all of our parts? Anyway, this is beyond me. There really is a God, and He did give us our existence. Putting Him into the equation seems to answer a whole lot of questions."

Caleb interrupted Bill's reflection. "Do you notice something different about space tonight?"

"What do you mean?" Bill asked, peering out into the darkness.

"It seems darker than before," Caleb commented.

Jack looked out too and noticed a gray cloud forming around Earth. "Something isn't right," Jack said. "It's as if the universe is losing its light and is being enveloped in darkness."

They stared out into the universe, thinking of home.

Jack continued, "Well, gentlemen, we have our last clue to solve to pass the test. We best get started, so we can get home."

"Let's find the rod in the Old Testament," Caleb said.

The three astronauts searched the Old Testament for several hours.

The Angel came to them once they had enough clues connecting the rod to the priesthood.

"We found clues in the Book of Numbers, in the story of the rod that budded," Caleb said to the Angel. "We read that the people of Israel challenged Moses and his brother, Aaron, about which tribe should take the priestly office. [37] God had each of the tribes write their name on a rod. The rod that budded first would be chosen for the priesthood.

"The following day, they found that Aaron's rod had budded and blossomed and even had ripe almonds on it. God had Moses put the rod

---

37 Nm 17:6–26.

in the Ark 'to be kept there as a warning to the rebellious so that their grumbling might cease before'[38] Him."

"What does the rod represent?" the Angel asked.

"In the Old Testament, the rod represents the priesthood," Caleb said, "and here, God chose the tribe of Levi, which Aaron was part of, to fulfill the priestly office."

"In the New Testament, in the Book of Hebrews," Jack added, "Saint Paul said, 'Where Jesus has entered on our behalf as forerunner, becoming high priest forever according to the order of Melchizedek.'"[39]

"That is correct. Jesus is the high priest in the New Testament," the Angel confirmed. "Now, let's summarize how these three clues take on life in the New Testament."

Jack listed the three items, and next to them, he defined what they meant in the Old and New Testament.

The Three Clues in the Ark	Old Testament (Symbol)	New Testament (Living Form)
1. The stone tablets	Word	Jesus is the Word of the Father made flesh.
2. The manna	Bread	Jesus is the living bread from Heaven.
3. The rod	Priest	Jesus is the high priest.

"All these clues point to Jesus," Bill said. "We learned that the Ark is Mary and that the items inside the Ark represent Jesus."

---

38 Nm 17:25.
39 Heb 6:20.

"That is correct, but what does this all mean? You need to find out *why* God left these clues, and what is the importance of the Ark and the items in the Ark in present time," the Angel said.

Caleb scratched his head and said, "So, we need to figure out God's motives and their importance of the items today?"

The Angel smiled and gave them additional help. "What do all these clues say about the Eternal Father? He went through all this trouble to create the Ark, so it must be significant. Ask yourself: what is the significance of the Ark of the Covenant in the present time? This will be your last test."

The Angel left them to ponder the Eternal Father's motives.

Then God's temple in Heaven was opened, and the Ark of His Covenant could be seen in the temple.

— Revelation 11:19

The Living Promise

BACK IN THEIR SPACE SHUTTLE, the astronauts pondered about what they discovered about the Ark, Jesus, and Mary.

Jack remembered visiting Jesus in the tabernacle back home. Without warning, the Angel transported Jack outside the Church of his childhood. The street was empty and the whole town, in fact, seemed to have fallen into a deep sleep. Not a sound could be heard. Even the hooting owls and chirping crickets had fled the scene, adding to the eerie silence. Jack stood alone under a waning moon staring at the Church. By its light, he saw wooden planks nailed to the Church doors and tacked to the planks read a sign in bold, black letters:

ST. MICHAEL THE ARCHANGEL CHURCH
CLOSED
by order of the U.S. Marshall
Violators will be imprisoned

Then, he heard the Angel's voice. "God is permitting you to see the future. Freedom to practice religion will be abolished. All religion will be brought down to its knees by a great evil mastermind and all will be forced to worship him."

Jack stood frozen, speechless. He walked around the side of the Church and peered inside through a stained-glass window. He saw pews flipped over and missals and song booklets hurled on the floor, the

Altar demolished. Hateful graffiti covered the walls. Behind the Altar was the tabernacle with its door ripped off and its contents emptied.

Sadness filled his heart, and he turned to the Angel who appeared beside him. "I was one of the lukewarm souls. I didn't keep God in my life. He wasn't important to me. Is it too late to change the events that are coming to the world?"

"God provided a weapon for the people to use, but they are not using it. But, It is not too late. As long as a soul is still alive, it has time. God waits, even to the last breath, for a soul to repent and return to Him," the Angel said.

This was the Church where his parents had made their vows, pronouncing them husband and wife. It was the same place that he and his wife repeated the same vows twenty-five years later. His mother's words came to him: *God will be with His people to the end of time. He made a covenant, a scared promise, like the marriage vows that your dad and I exchanged.*

"So, it's not too late. God never abandons His people. He made a promise, and He will fulfill it," Jack said with faith. In a moment, Jack was transported to the present.

After Jack came back to the ship, he went to look for his Rosary that his mother made him promise to keep close to him. His mother mentioned something else about the Hail Mary prayer, but he couldn't recall what it was. He went to Caleb and Bill to tell them what he learned.

"The Covenant!" Caleb blurted.

"What about the Covenant?" Bill asked. "Is it working again so we can fix the satellite?"

"No, I meant the Covenant God made with His people in the Old Testament," Caleb said.

"Yes, and he made it again in the New Testament," said Jack as he floated weightlessly toward them.

"What is this Covenant that He made?" Bill asked.

"He will always be with His people," Jack and Caleb said at the same time.

"Okay, that was too coincidental," said Bill.

Jack said, "Jesus is the Covenant that God made with the Israelites when He said, 'I will be with my people forever.' The Jews didn't know that God meant Jesus when He said that. God fulfilled this promise through Jesus in the Holy Eucharist."

Caleb said, "So all along Jesus came to fulfill the Father's promise to us."

"Do you mean that Jesus is the living form of God's covenant?" Bill asked.

"If the Jews knew this, they'd be converted," Caleb said, "Why did it take thousands of years for us to realize this?"

"The clues were all there, but it takes God to reveal them to us," Jack clarified, "If they come to understand *and* believe that God can be with His people to the end of time by turning bread into Himself in the Holy Eucharist, *then* they will be converted."

Do not think that I come to abolish the law or the prophets. I have come not to abolish but to fulfill.

— MATHEW 5:17

Bearers of a Great Treasure

WHILE THEY WAITED FOR THE Angel's next visit, the astronauts continued to discuss how well God placed clues and symbols throughout the centuries for mankind to find. They realized that God reveals things slowly through the ages and that each generation's under-standing of God grows and progresses as times goes on.

Bill saw Jack fingering a chain and asked, "What's that you're holding?"

"It was given to me by my mother. It's called the Rosary. Catholics use it to meditate on the Gospels about the lives of Jesus and Mary. She would pray the five decades of the Rosary every day."

"What are the five decades?" asked Bill.

"There are five decades in a Rosary. Each decade has ten beads, and on each bead, you say the Hail Mary prayer. The five decades are used to meditate on the sacred mysteries of Jesus's life. They include medita-tion on His birth, His proclamation of the Kingdom of God, His Passion and death on the Cross and His glorious resurrection," explained Jack.

"Interesting. Can I look at it? And what's the Hail Mary?" Bill asked.

Jack handed the Rosary to Bill and said, "The Hail Mary is a prayer taken from the Gospel of Luke from the words of Saint Gabriel and Elizabeth, the mother of John the Baptist."

"How does the prayer go?" asked Bill.

"It goes like this: 'Hail, Mary, full of grace. The Lord is with thee. Blessed art thou among women, and blessed is the fruit of thy womb,

Jesus. Holy Mary, Mother of God, pray for us sinners, now and at the hour of our death. Amen,'" Jack recited. He opened the Bible to the Gospel of Luke and showed Bill the words to the prayer.

"Hmm. Interesting," Bill said after he read Luke 1:28–44. "The Ark of the Covenant is Mary, and the items within it point to Jesus. The Hail Mary talks about Mary and the womb that holds Jesus. Don't they seem related?"

Jack looked at Bill, intrigued. Then, it came to him. "That's it! That's what my mother meant when she said, 'the Hail Mary prayer is the prayer of the Ark of the Covenant,'" Jack exclaimed. "Miracles come about from this prayer and the Rosary."

"You mean the Rosary has power similar to the Ark of the Covenant?" asked Bill.

"I think you might be right," said Jack.
"Then, the number five must have some meaning, because God seems to use numbers to communicate with us," Bill said.

"For an atheist, you sure are catching on fast—faster than we are," Caleb said.

Jack, Caleb, and Bill examined the significance of the Ark of the Covenant to the Hail Mary prayer, the Holy Eucharist, and the number five. The pieces were falling into place.

"I am beginning to like this God of yours," said Bill. "But how can a loving God allow hell to exist and punishment for eternity? It just doesn't make sense to me."

At that moment, the Angel of light appeared. Looking at Bill, the Angel said, "If the kings of Earth can have their dungeons and prisons to sentence those who do not follow their laws and who offend them, should not the King of the Universe have a place for those not in His favor?"[40]

"Huh, I never thought of it that way," responded Bill. The Angel added, "Time in the physical world is temporary. But, time in the spiritual world last for all eternity. Therefore hell is also eternal."

---

40 *The Dogma of Hell* by Rev Father F.X. Schouppe, S.J. p. 41.

The Angel turned to the other astronauts and said, "I would like to take you to one more place in Jerusalem." The astronauts found themselves on the second floor of a modest adobe home overlooking the city. The room was bare except for the long wooden table capable of seating many.

"It all started here in this room," said the Angel.

"What started in this room?" Jack asked.

"Jesus' mission," the Angel answered, "It was here in this upper room that He instituted the Mass, the Holy Eucharist, and the Priesthood."

Jack said with excitement. "Yes, the *mission* is the motive. Jesus's mission was to show the world His Father's love. It was a mission of love."

"The Ark of the Covenant and the items within it are God the Father's everlasting signs of His great love for His people," Bill added.

"Yes, go on," the Angel said.

"The Eternal Father loved His people so much that He made a perpetual promise that He would be with His people to the end of time,"[41] Caleb continued.

"He promised to be with them in good times and in bad, in sickness and in health, for richer or poorer," Jack chimed in. "The Ark of the Covenant was a token to remind the people of His promise."

Caleb said, "It was like a marriage vow. That is why God always referred to Himself as the groom and Israel as His beloved bride."

Bill said with great enthusiasm, "The Ark is Mary, and the Covenant is Jesus. That's why it is called the 'Ark of the Covenant.' God promised that He would be with His people. He fulfilled this promise through His Son. Through His Son, Jesus, God can be with His people until the end of time. Jesus is the Living Promise of God the Father."

The Angel interrupted. "And how will God be with His people until the end of time?"

Jack responded, "He will be with His people until the end of time in the Living Bread. God does this through the three items in the Ark."

"How so?" asked the Angel.

"At every Holy Sacrifice of the Mass," Jack explained, "three things are required to have God come down from Heaven.

---

41 Gn 26:3–5, 28:13–15; Mt 28:20.

They are the **Word**, the **bread,** and the **priest**. When the priest takes the bread and says the Words:

> *Take this, all of you, and eat of it, for "this is my*
> *Body, which will be given up for you."*[42]
> *And likewise the cup of wine saying,*
> *take this, all of you, and drink from it, "this cup is the new*
> *Covenant in my Blood, which will be shed for you and for many*
> *for the forgiveness of sins. Do this in memory of me."*[43]

At these supernatural[44] words, the bread and wine that the priest holds in his hands are no longer bread and wine but Jesus Himself. That is why the people kneel before the Body and Blood of Christ, which appear to be bread and wine.

---

42 Lk 22:19.

43 Lk 22:20.

44 The Words of Consecration are words Jesus himself spoke at the Last Supper when consecrating bread and wine during the Liturgy of the Holy Eucharistic.

"Yes, this is how God is with His people," the Angel said. "O, the dignity of the priesthood. Priests are ranked above all the kings of the Earth, for it is only through the priesthood that God transforms bread into His Flesh. Even the Blessed Mother, the Mother of God, is not given the honor of the priesthood. Wretched fools are the Judases within the Church, who do not realize their high station. No man will ever fully comprehend the privilege of this noble calling to be a priest of Christ."

Jack agreed; he hadn't truly appreciated the Mass or the Holy Eucharist. Now he fully understood this conversion of the Eucharistic elements into the Body and Blood of Christ.

Suddenly, Bill said, "I got it! The number five! Mathematics is used to explain science, right? Well, God left a clue with this Rosary of five decades."

"Yes, what about the number five?" asked the Angel.

"Well, David's five stones and the five decades of the Rosary have a connection," Bill said. "David took down Goliath with his stone, and the Ark crumbled the wall of Jericho and many other battles in the Old Testament. Well, then the Rosary is a weapon like David's five stones were."

The Angel smiled and said, "Yes, the stones and the Ark of the Covenant were weapons used in the Old Testament. The Rosary is a weapon in the hands of the faithful—just like the slingshot of David. The five decades call on Mary and Jesus, the Ark and the Covenant, to come into battle. So, the Rosary is the new weapon for the present age. God wants to put this powerful weapon into every person's hands. The Rosary is the weapon to battle Satan and his devils."

Jack clutched his Rosary and for the first time understood its value.

"Our Blessed Lady, Mary, has been pleading for mankind to pick up the Rosary and pray the prayers," the Angel responded. "Besides the Holy Eucharist and the Mass, the Rosary is the greatest weapon you can use to destroy Satan and his followers."

"My mom told me that the Rosary had power," said Jack, "but I didn't understand it, and I didn't pray it."

"Satan has planted the seeds of disbelief among the people about the Mother of God and her intercession for us with her Son. He does this to weaken the people's faith and to hinder the people from obtaining protection from their Heavenly Mother," explained the Angel.

Bill asked the Angel, "Did David really only use one small pebble to bring down this enormous man, Goliath? I read the story the other night and from a soldier's point of view, it just doesn't make sense."

The Angel said, "You are right that it was not by David's own strength and might that he defeated Goliath. He stood up for God and it was his trust in God that won him the victory. David was appalled that the Philistines were insulting his God, and that not even the fiercest warriors stood up for the Living God. David said to Goliath, "All... shall learn that it is not by sword or spear that the Lord saves. For the battle is the Lord's, and he shall deliver you into my hands."[45]

"So, David believed that God would battle for him?" Bill asked.

"Yes, Saul and his men responded with fear, but David responded with faith in God and knew that God would battle for him and hand him the victory. When the pebble hit Goliath's forehead, the Angel smote him for blaspheming the Lord. A miracle was given to David that day."

Bill wondered how many more battles he and his men could have won if they had God on their side.

The Angel said, "The Rosary can have the same effect as David's slingshot. The size of the weapon does not matter; it is the amount of faith which God uses to win battles."

Then, a bright light illuminated each of the three men.

The Angel said, "You now understand the Ark of the Covenant and have earned your stars." Three little stars danced above their heads and remained floating over them.

The Angel said, "These stars will be used for a special mission. They will join nine other stars for the Great Warning on Earth."

"The *other* nine stars?" the astronauts said at the same time.

---

45 1 Sm 17:47.

"Yes. The other nine stars represent the cooperation of those in times past, who have learned and passed the tests on the Ark of the Covenant's mystery. Together, the twelve stars represent the apostles for the end time."

The Angel then sent the stars to their mission. He said to the astronauts, "You have heard of the Star of Bethlehem. Just as the Star of Bethlehem shone brightly to guide the three wise men to Mary and the Baby Jesus, so these twelve stars are called to shine brightly, on the day of the Great Warning[46] so that all on Earth can see our Queen and the Child Jesus. Your mission is to tell what you have learned to those on Earth. Your satellite is working again. You may go home."

> *You are bearers of a great treasure. The devil knows its value. He considers it well worthwhile to rob you of it, and very often he does this in an instant… He sees you trying to work your way into the places of the fallen Cherubim and Seraphim; he is envious of you. Moreover, he attacks you so as to outmaneuver our Lord, "I cannot overthrow You," he seems to say to Jesus: "I will at least destroy these living ciboria of Yours." He avenges upon us his powerlessness against our Savior, Who overcame him.[47]*

— St. Peter Julian Eymard

---

46 *The Miracle of the Illumination of All Conscience,* by Thomas W. Petrisko, p.135.
47 *In the Light of the Monstrance,* by Saint Peter Julian Eymard, p. 7.

CHAPTER 19

Man of Peace

BACK ON THE FLIGHT DECK, the astronauts stared inquisitively at each other, each one's mind full of questions.

"This is a ridiculous question, but do you think that those three stars understood what the Angel was saying?" Bill asked, "Can stars talk?"

"Well, how much more ridiculous is it than when God spoke to Moses through a burning bush?" Caleb countered.

"After what we've been through, you should know that anything is possible with God," Jack said.

"Yes," Bill concurred. Then he sighed despondently, "I wish we could go back in time to see how God created the world."

"There are more things I want to know too. I would like Him to show us Heaven and see those who have passed away, like my mom." said Jack, "There is so much more we don't know."

"I used to think that the whole of creation began with the 'big bang,' but now I see that it was God who started the 'big bang.' The order and perfections of the universe aren't the results of chance but the work of a creator," Bill said.

"So, you're a believer now?" Caleb asked hopefully.

"You could say that." Bill responded with a smile.

A majestic light appeared before them. It was luminous and transcended all Earthly beauty, like the light they saw when they first met the Angel. However, this light was even more powerful and seemed to have come from God's own hands. This force compelled the three men to kneel, transfixed in awe at this wonder.

The glorious light slowly faded; its sunbeams dimmed to reveal a young woman more radiant than the sun. She was clothed in pure white. Her raven black hair was tucked under a blue mantle. She had deep, heavenly blue eyes, and skin like porcelain.

Our Lady said, "Children of my love. Thank you for having responded to my call. Now more than ever, my children need to turn back to God. The time of mercy is now, but soon God's justice will come since the sin of man has overflowed for too long. I am showing you the future."

She presented the three astronauts a vision of the future where world famine, diseases, and natural disasters ravaged the earth, devouring man and beast alike. They saw that a Great War did, indeed, break out on Earth. It was the most significant devastation of humankind ever, taking more lives than the holocaust and all previous wars combined. Then, a man appeared who seemed to have a solution to all the world's problems. He was charming, mesmerizing, and all the people were drawn to him. His speaking skills surpassed even the greatest orators, and his magnetic personality won all the people's hearts. But behind this whole façade of perfection was a wolf in sheep's clothing. In battle, he was mortally wounded and appeared to die. But he had staged his death and the people witnessed a hoax resurrection.

Our Lady said, "At this sight, man will abandon God because this man promised to restore the worldly goods and pleasures that they had lost. These deluded men and freethinkers will reinforce faith and will consider him their savior,[48] for he will bring unprecedented economic prosperity to all nations. Material wealth will overflow under his leadership. He will possess the power to send fire down from Heaven, move mountains, make objects speak, and transform demons into angels of light. Many will declare this man the Messiah they had been waiting for, because he will obtain peace for the world, uniting all

---

48 *The End of the Present World and the Mysteries of the Future Life* by Fr. Charles Arminjon, pp. 46-47.

nations and religions into one world order, with himself as the head. Christians whose faith is not deeply rooted in the truth will easily forget their belief in God and follow this man. This will open the door for him to take over all the temples and churches and command the whole world to worship him. The just will be dishonored and despised. They will be called fools and disturbers of the peace. They will be accused of trampling upon honor and patriotism by refusing to agree with the greatest man ever to have appeared in the world, the incomparable genius who raised human civilization to the zenith of perfection and progress.[49]

After the terrifying vision ended, the Lady said, "This powerful and wicked man, who many will raise to be the 'man of peace', will bring persecution to all who do not worship Satan. At about the same time, God will send two great witnesses: Enoch and Elijah, who were taken bodily into Heaven in the Old Testament to prophesy to the Truth to the people for 1,260 days.[51] They will be protected from persecution until their mission is accomplished; and then they will be martyred for their witness. The Jews will convert due to their prophecy and many will come back to God. Be not afraid, for in the end God's will for His Kingdom shall be accomplished."

Jesus said to them in reply, "See that no one deceives you. For many will come in my name, saying, 'I am the Messiah,' and they will deceive many. You will hear of wars and reports of wars; see that you are not alarmed, for these things must happen, but it will not yet be the end."

— MATTHEW 24:4

---

49 Ibid p. 49.

50 Ibid p. 53.

CHAPTER 20

Descending

OUR LADY CONTINUED, "YOU WILL be returning to Earth. Your eyes have been opened; go and tell the people what you have seen and learned. Within a short time after your return, the Great War will occur. The One World Order has already planted people into every fabric of society to help bring the Anti-Christ into the world. Many will follow and worship him.

Jack confirmed, "So, Jesus will come back to us on a cloud as He had when He ascended."

"Yes, if any man walking on Earth claims to be Jesus, you will know that the end is near. This imposter will deliberately contaminate Earth and inflict great spiritual devastation. He will force the mark of the beast upon the people to control them. Refuse this mark, for it brings a two-fold death—the death of the soul and the death of the body. Call out to your Guardian Angel who will guide you with a flame to a refuge; there you will stay for three and a half years. This will be the span of the reign of the anti-Christ. But, do not fear. God the Father never abandons His people, but the faithful will suffer much due to the sins of mankind."

"That will be hard to convince my people. The Jews rejected Jesus because they envisioned the Messiah as a worldly king who will unite all the nations under the Jews and bring prosperity and peace to the people. If this false Messiah can do all of that and perform great miracles, then I'm afraid that they will all believe this man is their savior," Caleb said.

"That is why you must pray, preach the good news and tell them about the true Messiah, Jesus, who has already walked the Earth. Thank you again for responding to my call and for the stars which you have helped to form." Then, she bid them Godspeed.

A voice from Command Center came through the speakers. "Come in, Covenant! Jack, are you there? Covenant, can you hear us?"

"Covenant responding!"

"Jack! It's so good to hear your voice! Are you all okay? How did you avoid the huge meteorite?"

"Long story, but we're happy to hear your voice! How long were we disconnected?" Jack asked.

"For about three hours, we were all so worried. We kept calling, hoping for a response. The satellite came on a few minutes ago, so we tried calling you again. Good work. You are all set to come home," Command Center relayed.

The three astronauts exchanged looks of astonishment. In three hours, they had time traveled and witnessed the most miraculous events in history; they had spoken to Angels, St. Joseph and the Mother of God. But most importantly, their outlook on life had changed and they would never be the same.

Upon their arrival at the Space Station, the astronauts had to adjust to the Earth's gravity again. Stepping out of the Space Station took some effort, but they were happy to be home. Once things were settled, they were updated on events that were happening on Earth while they were on their mission in space.

They learned that a pandemic started in the East and spread like wildfire to the entire world, resulting in the rapid deaths of thousands of people. In hearing this, the astronauts knew that this was just the begin-ning, as global economic instability and many other natural disasters had to occur before the rise of the evil one. They knew that they could not stop what is coming; but they could warn the people to prepare their souls and have faith in God.

One of the first things Jack did was visit his Church now that he valued the gift of Jesus' presence in the Holy Eucharist. He wanted to take advantage of it before it would be taken away. Caleb visited his Rabbi to explain the extraordinary relationship between the Ark of the Covenant in the Torah and the Bible to see if he could forewarn the Jews. Bill went home and was greeted by his girlfriend Linda. She cried upon seeing him. He looked at her then at her stomach and wondered if she did what he asked her to do several weeks before going on his mission.

She tenderly touched her stomach and said, "I couldn't do it. I couldn't abort our baby."

Bill said with tears welling in his eyes, "Thank you for not listening to me. I was so wrong." He looked up to Heaven and said, "Thank you, God, for keeping our baby safe."

Linda was relieved. "She's four-months-old. Can we name her Emily?" Bill was overjoyed. He grabbed her in his arms and said, "Yes, Emily is a beautiful name! Let's get married and be the parents she deserves." Days later, the three astronauts were seen on TV telling the world what happened in space and relaying the messages they received from St. Joseph and Our Lady.

This Jesus who has been taken up from you into Heaven will return in the same way as you have seen Him going into Heaven.

— ACTS 1:11

CHAPTER 21

The Father's Love

IN HEAVEN, THE QUEEN WENT to visit her Father. She saw Him once more looking through the eye of a needle. It was here that God the Father sees the world. Blood was dripping from this opening more than usual. She took a deep breath and closed her eyes in deep sadness.

It has been said that it is easier for a camel to pass through the eye of a needle than for a rich man to enter the kingdom of Heaven.[51] For the eye of a needle represents the wounds of Christ—it is the way of the Cross which redeems the world.

The Father held His Son's hands and said, "My Son, how long must I look through your wounds and wait for my children on Earth to come back to me?"

Blood dripped profusely from Jesus' wounds in reparation for the sins of man and He said, "Father, have mercy on them for they know not what they do."

The Father continued, "Because you have suffered for love of them, I will give them a great warning so that they can see their actions through Our eyes. I will shine my light through Your wounds and envelop mankind in it so that they may see the Truth. It is the way by which they can come to us. You, my Son, are the Way, the Truth, and the Life. They must know that My Mercy is infinite and that

---

51 Matt: 19:24.

I will always forgive them. All they need to do is acknowledge Me, Call out My name and I will come. Even if they committed all the sins of the world, if they trust in My mercy and ask for forgiveness, I will give it to them," the Father confirmed.

"I pray, Father, that the world comes to know that You sent Me and that they come to know You. May they all be one as We are one so that one day We will gather to rejoice in Your love and mercy," Jesus prayed.

The Queen knew that the Father knows all things, but she reminded Him of the astronauts' conversion upon learning the truth.

The Father smiled and said, "There is still hope for mankind once the truth is revealed."

Then, she requested if she could be sent to Earth again to warn the people.

"My daughter, you have appeared numerous times around the globe and they have not listened to your plea. Your statues have even shed tears of blood and they still turned deaf ears to your pleading. Lucifer, who chose at the beginning to become a beast, would not accept you as the Mother of God or the Queen of Heaven and Earth. This is the same for his followers, but I am happy to see that you have not given up on Our children. Your efforts will not be in vain."

The Lady thanked her Father and left to prepare for the Great Warning.

Do not fear, for "at the end of the world and in deed presently, because the Most High and His Holy Mother has to form for Himself great saints who shall surpass most of the other saints in sanctity. [...] These great souls, full of grace and zeal, shall be chosen to match themselves against the enemies of God, who shall rage on all sides..." [52]

— St. Louis De Montfort

---

52 *True Devotion to Mary* by St. Louis De Montfort, pp. 26-27 (#47-48).

"[...] *I saw a great radiance, and in the midst of it, God the Father. Between this radiance and the Earth, I saw Jesus nailed to the Cross in such a way that when God wanted to look at the Earth, He had to look through the wounds of Jesus. And I understood that it was for the sake of Jesus that God blesses the Earth.*"

— Diary of St. Faustina, #60

CHAPTER 22

Fourth Trumpet

Their Two Hearts are but one Ark of the Covenant

TIME WILL SOON FADE INTO Eternity, never to return. As the sufferings and tribulations increase, each person was confronted with a choice that would determine their eternal destiny. Seeing that the children of Earth had fallen even further from the truth, God commanded the Guardian of the Fourth Trumpet to sound the alarm throughout the universe.

The Angel of the Cosmos took a crown of twelve stars to meet the Queen.

The Queen had been anticipating his arrival. The Angel knelt before the Queen and presented the stars to her.

"My Lady, this is the Crown of Twelve Stars for the Great Warning."

He released the twelve stars out of his hands. They flew toward the Queen and formed a crown around her head. The light from the stars illuminated the Queen. The twelve stars represented the twelve tribes of Israel and the twelve Apostles. Now, at the end of time, they represented the raising of new apostles.

The Queen thanked the Angel and said, "God Almighty has permitted me one last appearance to my children on Earth. I pray that they will heed this final warning."

The humans were at war. It was the most destructive war ever, with nations battling against nations and using the most destructive weapons science could create, resulting in the instantaneous loss of millions of lives. The Queen could not sit still anymore. She had to intercede for her children. Within an instant, she was hovering over Earth with the Child Jesus on her right arm. Mother and Child looked down on the battlefield and were greatly saddened by the scene.

As they looked down upon Earth, they witnessed horrible destruction and the shedding of needless blood.

Look at them down there. They are blood related from Adam and Eve and they are killing their brothers and sisters. War is the universal effect of sin. Those who died never knew that death was coming and did not even have time to call out to God to repent. The Queen sorrowfully moaned as she saw millions of souls falling into Hell since their chance for repentance was taken from them. Tears streamed down her face and the face of the Infant Child. A sword of sorrow pierced Mary's heart, as was foretold by Simeon.[53] God the Father would soon use the Queen's pierced heart and the Sacred Heart of Jesus to reveal His thoughts to many.

The Angels of the Cosmos made the sun dance. For several minutes, the sun flickered as it bounced in all directions. Everyone on Earth looked up and was shocked as the sun came closer to them.

They screamed, "It's the end of the world!"

The war that had taken so many lives came to a stand still. The nations subsided their deployment of missiles and bombs for this moment.

Then, the sun went back up in the sky. It enveloped the Queen and the Infant Child with its light. The moon positioned itself under the Queen's feet, and the Crown of Twelve Stars encircled the Queen's head.

Some of the people did not run from the dancing sun but stood firm. They gazed at the sun with hopeful countenances. A man on Earth pointed to the sky and shouted, "I see a woman clothed with the sun, with the moon under her feet, on her head,

---

53 Lk 2:35.

a crown of twelve stars,[54] and on her arm is a Child!"

Overshadowing the Queen and the Infant Child was the cloud of glory, the Holy Spirit. The Holy Spirit sent rays of light through the Infant Child's Sacred Heart and the Queen's Immaculate Heart, right through to each person on Earth.

Everything froze in time. That Holy light revealed God's thoughts to His people. Each person saw how God viewed their souls. Each soul was given a review of their entire life. A summation of every good and evil deed was recorded in the Book of Life. This illumination of the soul is God's Divine Mercy on His people, giving them one last chance to repent. This was the fulfillment of Simeon's prophecy when he said to Mary, "A sword will pierce through your own soul also, so that thoughts from many hearts may be revealed."

---

54 Rv 12:1.

This was the people's last chance to choose. Either their souls would draw closer to God or be propelled further into the darkness. The time was near, and the separation of good and evil had begun.[55]

Another Angel came out of the temple, crying out in a loud voice to the one sitting on the cloud. "Use your sickle and reap and harvest, for the time to reap has come because the Earth's harvest is fully ripe."

— REVELATION 14:15

---

55 *The Final Battle for the Kingdom,* by T.L. Smith, p. 63

CHAPTER 23

Which Eternity?

THE QUEEN HELD OUT THE beaded chain to tell her children to take up battle, armed with the prayer of the Rosary. Saint Joseph appeared next to the Queen. Saint Joseph and the Infant Child raised their hands and blessed the world. Then, they disappeared from the sky and took their places back in Heaven.

Once the illuminating light left Earth, the world was left to contemplate this supernatural event. Many rejoiced over this miracle, but many others whose hearts denied God's existence chose to find ways to explain away this phenomenon. The phenomenon of the dancing sun reminded many of a similar event in Fatima.

In 1917, Our Lady, Queen of the Rosary, appeared to three children in Fatima, Portugal. In her third appearance to them on July 13, 1917, Lucia, one of the three children, described the vision of Hell that was shown to them:

> As Our Lady spoke these last words, she opened her hands once more, as she had done during the two previous months. The rays of light seemed to penetrate the earth, and we saw as it were a sea of fire. Plunged in this fire were demons and souls in human form, like transparent burning embers, all blackened or burnished bronze, floating about in the conflagration, now raised into the air by the flames that issued from within themselves together with great clouds of smoke now falling back on every side like sparks in huge fires, without

weight or equilibrium, amid shrieks and groans of pain and despair, which horrified us and made us tremble with fear. (It must have been this sight which caused me to cry out, as people say they heard me). The demons could be distinguished by their terrifying and repellent likeness to frightful and unknown animals, black and transparent like burning coals. Terrified and as if to plead for succor, we looked up at Our Lady, who said to us, so kindly and so sadly: *You have seen hell where the souls of poor sinners go. To save them, God wishes to establish in the world devotion to my Immaculate Heart. If what I say to you is done, many souls will be saved and there will be peace.*[56]

Several months before the Great Warning, Jack, Caleb, and Bill were interviewed by a Catholic news station. The three astronauts sat on a couch across from the news anchor, Elizabeth.

Elizabeth: "Thank you so much for taking this time to tell the world of your miraculous experiences in space. We heard that some extraordinary events took place in space and that you've come back with a message for the world. Let me start with you, Captain Jack Benson. Can you share with us your experience in space, how it changed your life, and what message you have to share with us?"

Jack: "Yes, well... where do I start."

Elizabeth: "Let's start with your childhood and your faith life growing up."

Jack: "Well, I was born and raised in a Catholic family. My mom was very committed to her faith and I still remember her teachings to this day. But I drifted away from the faith in college, and it wasn't till this mission that I encountered God and understood the importance of my faith for the first time."

After each of the astronauts shared their faith life before God's intervention on the space ship, along with how they solved the mystery

56 https://www.ncregister.com/blog/joseph-pronechen/fatima-july-13-apparition-ways-to-overcome-a-frightening-vision

of the Ark of the Covenant, it was time for them to reveal God's message to the world, the one St. Joseph had told them.

Jack: St. Joseph revealed to us the following: "The cloud of darkness will inevitably envelop the world, and light will be extinguished. Earth will experience three days of complete and utter darkness. This darkness will be worse than the loss of sight. Their hearts will be heavy and filled with fear from the empty void where God seems to no longer exist.

God will send the Angels of the World, the Archangels, and the Guardian Angels, to seal the faithful with the Cross of Jesus Christ. The Angels will seal the faithful remnants by signing an invisible Cross on their foreheads. At the same time, Satan will mark those who swore allegiance to him with the Mark of the Beast.

Many of those sealed for God will be called to martyrdom. When the time comes, the Angels will strengthen them to die for God and their names will be written in the Book of Life. Those whom God spares will be hidden in dens from the eyes of the beast and his cohorts. The hour will come like a thief in the night for those who have not prepared their souls."

Caleb: St. Joseph mentioned refuges, he said, "The Archangels have also prepared places of refuge for the coming tribulations. Soon, the Sacrifice of the Mass will be banned and the faithful will have to seek shelter underground and in hidden places prepared by God's people and His Angels.

It is man's free will or more precisely his choices that sways the balance of the forces of good and evil. As man gives his free will to the beast, the forces of evil gain more power. Once the people realize their misguided desires, they will call upon the True God to help destroy the beast they had worshiped."

Bill: He also said, "After the Great Warning, the people will be given forty days to repent. At the end of the Great Warning period, the time of mercy will end, and the time of justice will begin. Satan and his cohorts will take over, and they will reign over Earth for three and a half years. It will be a time of great tribulation. God, through the Queen and her Angels, has given man the means to defeat these creatures from Hell."

Caleb: "We must not fear, but trust that in the end, God's will be done. His battle plan– the Bible –tells us that those who choose God and persevere to the end will win. In the meantime, we need to heed our Queen's warning and prepare our souls. In the Final Battle for the Kingdom, the world will be pulled into a confrontation with the greatest enemy of mankind. In this Final Battle, the treasure is the human soul."[57]

Jack concluded the interview: "God has given us many weapons to fight this battle they include: praying the Rosary, fasting, penance, and; making use of the Seven Sacraments: Baptism, Confirmation, Eucharist, Penance, Anointing of the Sick, Holy Orders, and Matrimony. It's up to us to use them.

...Thy kingdom come, Thy will be done on Earth as it is in Heaven. God the Father so loved the world that He gave His only son to die and save us. To whom would you rather give your love and serve? Love is a choice. Just as it was in the beginning for the Angels to choose for or against God. It shall be the same for us in the end to choose for or against God. You have seen how Jesus, the mediator between God and man, fulfilled the Covenant foretold in the Old Testament and became the Living Covenant in the New Testament. The proof of God's love for us is visible in each person's life but you have to look for God and find the connections just as we did here with the Ark of the Covenant.

Time is of the essence. God the Father of Life is waiting in Heaven with love for you, while the Father of Death and Lies is waiting in Hell for you. Choose well; the battle for your soul is waging and is already at your door. Your eternal life depends on it. The choice is yours.

---

57 *The Final Battle for the Kingdom,* by T.L. Smith

FROM NASA TO THE PRIESTHOOD

IN THE BOOK, *HEALING THROUGH the Mass*, there is a story regarding a research scientist at NASA who became a priest after he encountered an event during the research with a Kirlian photography camera. The man "was a research scientist at NASA, working with a camera that could gauge and measure the aura of light around a human body [...]. NASA sought to identify and monitor the astronauts' aura in orbit to determine what was happening to them internally. They found that dying people have a very thin aura, like blue light, which gets weaker and weaker until they die.

The scientist and an associate were in a hospital behind a two-way mirror monitoring the aura of a dying man. As they watched, another man came into the room and filled the room with light emanating from his pocket. The man reached into his pocket and did something that caused the camera to be so filled with light that they could not see what was happening. They ran into the room only to discover the man giving Holy Communion to the dying man. They raced back to the camera and observed that as the dying man received Communion, his aura grew stronger.

After seeing this Eucharistic Miracle, the scientist knew that there was a higher power—that there was someone to be reckoned with, someone for whom he had to live his life. He left his job at NASA and became a Catholic priest.

Once we believe in something, once we see something deeply, we have a responsibility to act on those beliefs and be accountable for those actions. "When much has been given a man, much will be required of him (Lk 12:48)."[58]

There are many other great Eucharistic Miracles that you can research. I recommend reading about the Eucharistic Miracle that took place in the 8th century A.D. in Lanciano, Italy. This Eucharistic Miracle still exists today and scientists throughout the centuries are dumbfounded by this extraordinary phenomenon.

---

58 *Healing Through the Mass*, by Grandis De Robert, S.S. J. with Linda Schubert. pp. 84–85.

THE GREAT WARNING

THE GREAT WARNING WILL COME. It is God's mercy for the children of Earth. It is His last wake-up call. If you live to experience this warning, don't run from God. Instead, run to God and acknowledge His existence. Ask for His forgiveness and thank Him for His love. We have a loving God, and He wants you to join Him in heaven. Receive His love!

SAINT FAUSTINA DESCRIBES GOD'S MERCY

"Today I heard the words: **In the Old Covenant I sent prophets wielding thunderbolts to My people. Today I am sending you with My Mercy to the people of the whole world. I do not want to punish aching mankind, but I desire to heal it, pressing it to My Merciful Heart. I use punishment when they themselves force Me to do so; My hand is reluctant to take hold of the sword of justice. Before the Day of Justice, I am sending the Day of Mercy."**[59]

What does Mary mean when she says, "One day, My Immaculate Heart will triumph"?

"Only when Mary is understood can Christ, as God-Man, be understood. Only when we understand the action of the Holy Spirit in Mary, for the God-Man's incarnation, can we understand His relation to each of us.

"The triumph of the Sacred Heart will come only with the triumph of the Immaculate Heart of His Mother. The triumph of the Holy Spirit

---

59 *Diary of Saint Maria Faustina Kowalska: Divine Mercy in My Soul*, #1588.

will come only with the triumph of His spouse, the Mother of Jesus. When she said, 'My Immaculate Heart will triumph,' she was speaking of the triumph of her Son and of her Spouse."[60]

"Just as the Son, to show us how great his love is, became a man, so too the third Person, God-who-is-Love, willed to show his mediation as regards the Father and the Son by means of a concrete sign. This sign is the heart of the Immaculate Virgin...spouse of the Holy Spirit."[61]

SINS AGAINST THE IMMACULATE HEART OF MARY

Father Jose Bernardo Goncalves, S.J. asked Sister Lucia regarding the Five First Saturday devotion. He asked, "Why should it be five Saturdays and not nine or seven in honor of the sorrows of our Lady?"

God revealed this to Sr. Lucia. "Daughter, the motive is simple. There are five kinds of offenses and blasphemies spoken against the Immaculate Heart of Mary: blasphemies (1) against her Immaculate Conception; (2) against her perpetual virginity; (3) against her divine maternity, refusing at the same time to accept her as the Mother of mankind; (4) by those who try publicly to implant in the hearts of children indifference, contempt, and even hate for this Immaculate Mother; and (5) for those who insult her directly in her sacred images."[62]

THE ROSARY AND THE SCAPULAR

Pope Pius XII has said, "Sister Lucia pointed out [that] the scapular is our sign of consecration to the Immaculate Heart of Mary . . . the Scapular and the Rosary are inseparable.'"[63]

---

60 *Deadline: The Third Secret of Fatima,* by John M. Haffert, p. 51.
61 *The Marian Option,* Carrie Gress, PhD, p. 122.
62 *Fatima for Today,* Fr. Andrew Apostoli, C.F.R., pp. 156-157.
63 *Ibid*, p. 221.

Our Lady of Fatima said, "Through the Rosary and the Scapular, I will save the world."

Let us pray to understand the weapons we are to use against Satan and his cohorts. If the entire world were annihilated by man's weapons, such as nuclear bombs or chemical warfare, Satan and his cohorts would still exist. The only way to destroy these spiritual beings is with spiritual weapons. Through Mary, God the Father has given us these spiritual weapons. They are the Rosary and the Scapular. We ought to make use of them to protect ourselves and those we love.

PRAYER OF CONSECRATION TO JESUS THROUGH MARY

I, (*INSERT YOUR NAME*), A faithless sinner, renew and ratify today in thy Heart, O Immaculate Mother, the vows of my Baptism; I renounce forever Satan, his pomps and works; and I give myself entirely to Jesus Christ, the Incarnate Wisdom, to carry my cross after Him all the days of my life, and to be more faithful to Him than I have ever been before.

Queen of the Most Holy Rosary, in the presence of all the heavenly court, I choose thee this day for my Mother and Queen. I deliver and consecrate to thee, and to thy Immaculate Heart, as thy child and slave of love, my body and soul, my goods, both interior and exterior, and even the value of all my good actions, past, present and future; leaving to thee the entire and full right of disposing of me, and all that belongs to me, without exception, according to thy good pleasure, for the greater glory of God, in time and in eternity. Amen.

PRAYER FOR SPIRITUAL COMMUNION

My Jesus, I believe that You
are present in the Most Holy Sacrament.
I love You above all things, and I desire to receive You into my soul.
Since I cannot at this moment receive You sacramentally,
come at least spiritually into my heart.
I embrace You as if You were already there
and unite myself wholly to You.
Never permit me to be separated from You.
Amen.

BEST PRAYER FOR THE END TIMES PSALM 91

You who dwell in the shelter of the Most High,
who abide in the shade of the Almighty,
2 Say to the LORD, "My refuge and fortress,
my God in whom I trust."
3 He will rescue you from the fowler's snare,
from the destroying plague,
4 He will shelter you with his pinions,
and under his wings you may take refuge;
his faithfulness is a protecting shield.
5 You shall not fear the terror of the night
nor the arrow that flies by day,
6 Nor the pestilence that roams in darkness,
nor the plague that ravages at noon.
7 Though a thousand fall at your side,
ten thousand at your right hand,
near you it shall not come.
8 You need simply watch;
the punishment of the wicked you will see.
9 Because you have the LORD for your refuge
and have made the Most High your stronghold,
10 No evil shall befall you,
no affliction come near your tent.

*11 For he commands his Angels with regard to
you, to guard you wherever you go.*
*12 With their hands they shall support you,
lest you strike your foot against a stone.*
*13 You can tread upon the asp and the viper,
trample the lion and the dragon.*
*14 Because he clings to me I will deliver him;
because he knows my name I will set him on high.*
*15 He will call upon me and I will answer;
I will be with him in distress;
I will deliver him and give him honor.*
*16 With length of days I will satisfy him,
and fill him with my saving power.*

SEVEN TRUMPETS
OF THE BIBLE

The First Trumpet - Rev 8:7
"When the first one blew his trumpet, there came hail and fire mixed with blood, which was hurled down to the earth. A third of the land was burned up, along with a third of the trees and all green grass."

The Second Trumpet - Rev 8:8-9
"When the second Angel blew his trumpet, something like a large burning mountain was hurled into the sea. A third of the sea turned to blood, a third of the creatures living in the sea died, and a third of the ships were wrecked."

The Third Trumpet - Rev 8:10-11
"When the third Angel blew his trumpet, a large star burning like a torch fell from the sky. It fell on a third of the rivers and on the springs of water. The star was called "Wormwood," and a third of all the water turned to wormwood. Many people died from this water because it was made bitter."

The Fourth Trumpet - Rev 8:12
"When the fourth Angel blew his trumpet, a third of the sun, a third of the moon, and a third of the stars were struck, so that a third of them became dark. The day lost its light for a third of the time, as did the night."

The Fifth Trumpet - Rev 9:1-2
"Then the fifth Angel blew his trumpet, and I saw a star that had fallen from the sky to the earth. It was given the key for the passage to the abyss. It opened the passage to the abyss, and smoke came up out of the passage like smoke down a huge furnace. The sun and the air were darkened by the smoke from the passage."

The Sixth Trumpet - Rev 9:13-15
"Then the sixth Angel blew his trumpet.... Release the four Angels who were bound at the banks.... So the four Angels were released, who were

prepared for this hour, day, month, and year to kill a third of the human race."

The Seventh Trumpet - Rev 10:15

"Then the seventh Angel blew his trumpet. There were loud voices in heaven, saying, 'The kingdom of the world now belongs to our Lord and to his Anointed, and he will reign forever and ever.

G L O S S A R Y

Abomination of Desolation: The "horrible abomination" is also known as the "Abomination of Desolation" (see Daniel 12:11–12; Matthew 24:15–21, and Mark 13:14–19). The Abomination of Desolation is the elimination of the Most Holy Eucharist, the Most Precious Body and Blood of Our Lord, Jesus Christ, from the Holy Mass and Holy Tabernacles. It is the invalid consecration by a priest whereby the bread and wine are not transformed into Our Lord, Jesus Christ.

Commandments: "In this, we know that we love the children of God: when we love God and keep His commandments." — 1 JOHN 5:2

"And the dragon was angry against the woman and went to make war with the rest of her seed, who keep the commandments of God, and have the testimony of Jesus Christ." — REVELATION 12:17

> **The Ten Commandments:** The first three Commandments are about the love of God, and the remaining seven Commandments are about the love of neighbors.
>
> 1. I am the Lord your God; You shall not have other gods before me.
> 2. You shall not take the Lord's name in vain.
> 3. Remember to keep holy the Lord's Day.
> 4. Honor your Father and your Mother.
> 5. You shall not kill.
> 6. You shall not commit adultery
> 7. You shall not steal.
> 8. You shall not bear false witness against your neighbor.
> 9. You shall not covet your neighbor's wife.
> 10. You shall not covet your neighbor's goods.

Covenant: "A covenant is like a contract, but it is much more than merely a contract. A covenant establishes bonds of sacred kinship... God's covenant unites persons in a union that is meant to be lasting."[64]

The seven covenants between God and us in salvation history:[65]

1. God's covenant with Adam (Gn 1: 26–30)
2. God's Covenant with Noah (Gn 9:1–17)
3. God's Covenant with Abraham (Gn 12:1–3)
4. The Mosaic Covenant (Ex 24:3–8, 19: 3–8)
5. God's Covenant with David (2 Sm 7:12–13)
6. The New Covenant with Christ (Matt 26:26, Luke 22:20)
7. At the end time, the general resurrection, comes the fulfillment of the New Covenant.

Eternal Laws: Laws that are unchanging and eternal in nature because they are God's laws. The Ten Commandments are laws revealed by God and are eternal.

Great Warning: The Great Warning is God's mercy to draw us closer to Him and to increase our faith. It is God's last call before He comes as a just judge. St. Faustina says in her Diary, "This is the time of Mercy." ~ Diary of St. Faustina #83, 441, 1058, 1107, and 1588

Hell: "It is a place of great torture [...]. Here each soul undergoes terrible and indescribable sufferings, related to the manner in which it has sinned [...]. Let the sinner know that he will be tortured throughout eternity, in those senses which he made use of to sin." ~ Diary of St. Faustina, #741

> "You have but two final destinies: Heaven and Hell. Know that Satan will try to remove the reality of the existence of his kingdom, Hell, from you. If he makes a farce of his existence among you, he will deceive you so that you will sin and remove yourselves from the Spirit of Light. And when you remove yourselves from the Spirit of Light, you remove yourselves from eternal life in the Kingdom of your Father, the Most High God in Heaven."
> — Our Lady, February 1, 1975

Illumination: Knowledge revealed to us by the Holy Spirit that we would not ordinarily be able to comprehend (e.g., the teachings of the Holy Trinity.

Mass: "The celebration of the Eucharist is often called 'the holy sacrifice of the Mass' [...]. [It] does not merely recall a past event. It makes the event present."[66] Read, *A Biblical Walk Through the Mass* by Dr. Edward Sri to learn about the beauty of the Mass.

    Per the Catechism of the Catholic #1330 The *memorial* of the Lord's Passion and Resurrection.

> The *Holy Sacrifice,* because it makes present the one sacrifice of Christ the Savior and includes the Church's offering. The terms *holy sacrifice of the Mass,* "*sacrifice of praise,*" *spiritual sacrifice, pure and holy sacrifice* are also used,[150] since it completes and surpasses all the sacrifices of the Old Covenant.

Natural Laws: Saint Thomas Aquinas explains that Natural Law is man's participation in the Eternal Law. Its general precept is that "good is to be done and pursued, and evil is to be avoided."

---

66 A Biblical Walk Through the Mass by Edward Sri, p. 7–8.

Nine Choirs of Angels: There are nine orders of Angels. Each order has its own office, or position of authority. The angels are listed in three orders of three, as follows, with the Seraphim being the highest order:[67]

Angels of Pure Contemplation (Govern all Creation)
I.   1. Seraphim
     2. Cherubim
     3. Thrones

Angels of the Cosmos (Govern All the Cosmos)
II. 4. Dominions
     5. Virtues
     6. Powers

Angels of the World (Govern all the World)
III. 7. Principalities
     8. Archangels
     9. Angels

Purgatory: "There is a purgatory, a place of purging, my child—suffering great as in the abyss, but with the knowledge of a reprieve in time to come. It is a bleak longing of the spirit to look upon the Father. Know, my child, this longing of the heart in the fires is of great magnitude encompassing the being of the waiting soul." ~ Our Lady, March 29, 1975

Purity: "Unless you keep pure and holy thoughts in your mind and keep your body clean, you cannot enter into the Kingdom of Heaven! Your body is the temple of your eternal spirit! Your eyes are the mirror for your soul!" ~ Our Lady, July 25, 1974

---

67 *Angel Power* by Janice Connelly, p. 10.

Sacrament: A Sacrament is an outward sign instituted by Christ to give There are seven Sacraments: Baptism, Penance (Confession), Holy Eucharist (Holy Communion), Confirmation, Matrimony, Holy Orders, Extreme Unction (Last Rites).

Tabernacle: The receptacle in which the Blessed Sacrament is reserved in Churches, chapels, and oratories. It is to be immovable, solid, locked, and located in a prominent place. Sister Lucy of Fatima said, "Mary is the first living tabernacle where the Father enclosed His Word. Her Immaculate Heart is the first monstrance that sheltered Him. Her lap and her arms were the first altar and the first throne upon which the Son of God made man was adored."

Words of Consecration: The words used by Jesus to transform the bread and wine into His Body and Blood. To transform the bread and wine into Jesus's Body, Blood, Soul and Divinity, the priest must say, "This is my Body" and "This is my Blood" over the bread and wine, respectively.

Per the Catechism of the present in this sacrament. The Church Fathers strongly affirmed the faith of the Church in the efficacy of the Word of Christ and of the action of the Holy Spirit to bring about this conversion. Thus St. John Chrysostom declares:

It is not man that causes the things offered to become the Body and Blood of Christ, but he who was crucified for us, Christ himself. The priest, in the role of Christ, pronounces these words, but their power and grace are God's. **"This is my Body," he says. This word transforms the things offered.**

#1376   The Council of Trent summarizes the Catholic faith by declaring: "Because Christ our Redeemer said that it was truly his Body that he was offering under the species of bread, it has always been the conviction of the the Church of God, and this holy council now declares again, that by the consecration of the bread and wine there takes place a change of the whole substance of the bread into the substance of the body of Christ our Lord and of the whole substance of the wine into the substance of his blood. This change the holy Catholic Church has fittingly and properly called transubstantiation."

BIBLIOGRAPHY

Apostoli, Father Andrew, C.F.R. *Fatima for Today the Urgent Marian Message of Hope*. San Francisco: Ignatius Press, 2010.

Arminjon, Father Charles. *The End of the Present World and the Mysteries of the Future Life*. Manchester, New Hampshire: Sophia Institute Press, 2008.

Connell, Janice J. *Angel Power*. New York: Ballantine Books, 1995.

C.S. Lewis, *The Screwtape Letters*. New York: Harper One, 2000.

De Montfort, St. Louis-Marie Grignion. *True Devotion to Mary*. Rockford, Illinois: TAN Books and Publishers, Inc., 1985.

Faustina Kowalska, Maria. *Diary of Saint Maria Faustina Kowalska: Divine Mercy in My Soul*. Massachusetts: Marian Press, 2014.

Fr. F. X. Schouppe, S.J. The Dogma of Hell, Charlotte, North Caroline: TAN Books, an Imprint of Saint Benedict, LLC, 2012.

Grandis, De Robert, S.S. J. and Schubert, Linda. *Healing Through the Mass*. Resurrection Press, an Imprint of Catholic Book Publishing, Corp. Totowa, New Jersey.

Gress, Carrie. *The Marian Option*. Charlotte, North Carolina: TAN Books, 2017

Haffert, John M. *Deadline: The Third Secret of Fatima*.

Haffert, John M. *Her Own Words to the Nuclear Age: The Memoirs of Sr. Lucia*. New Jersey: The 101 Foundation, Inc., 1993.

Hahn, Scott, Ph D . *Understanding The Scriptures: A Complete Course On Bible Study.* The Didache Series.

Salve Maria Regina.info. "The Message of Fatima," in *Highlights of Our Lady of Fatima's Message to the World.*

Petrisko, Thomas. *The Miracle of the Illumination of All Consciences* Pennsylvania: St. Andrew's Productions, 2002.

Smith, T.L. *The Final Battle for the Kingdom.* JMJYoungReaders.com, 2016.

Sri, Edward. *A Biblical Walk Through the Mass: Understanding What We Say and Do in the Liturgy.* Pennsylvania: Ascension Press, 2011.

Sri, Edward. *Love Unveiled: The Catholic Faith Explained.* San Francisco: Ignatius Press, 2015.

The Father Speaks to His Children. "Pater" Publications, 4th edition in English, October 7, 1999.